The Masters Review

ten stories

Volume IV

Courtney Bird · Sarah Smith · Adam Gardner
Megan Clark · Christina Milletti
CB Anderson · H. L. Nelson · Joe Dornich
Daniel Bullard-Bates · Jennifer Stern

Stories Selected by Kevin Brockmeier
Edited by Kim Winternheimer and Sadye Teiser

Editor's Note

I am so pleased to share with you the fourth volume of *The Masters Review*, with stories selected by Kevin Brockmeier.

Each year our staff deliberates over queries to guest judges, looking for a writer with a point of view that brings something new to the collection. Kevin Brockmeier's works are literary, genre, memoir, science fiction, and so many wonderful things all at once, we were thrilled when he agreed to participate. We add him to a growing list of established authors who offer a wonderful endorsement to the writers featured in our anthologies.

This year we opened submissions to emerging writers of all kinds, not just those in graduate-level programs. As *The Masters Review* grows in its literary pursuits, its focus remains on celebrating and promoting new authors. Yet, by showcasing writers from a single demographic we were limiting our platform. As we mark our fourth year, we are thrilled to embrace a growing range of voices. This year we published fiction from Kate Bernheimer, Ben Loory, Manuel Gonzales, and Ben Hoffman, all alongside work from emerging writers. Some of those new writers went on to earn selections from *The Best of The Net* anthology and *The Best Small Fictions*. Last year's book won an INDIEFAB silver medal for best short story collection and provided a platform that was successful in connecting many of our authors with agents. We offer as much as we can to our writers and to our readership, because we believe the sense of community in the literary world is at the heart of how new writers begin and how established authors continue.

We received more submissions this year than in our anthology's history, and the ten stories you read here reflect a diverse and exciting group. There were no nonfiction pieces selected, though we saw a number of quality essays, many of which made the shortlist. And while we continue to champion narrative nonfiction, this year's anthology is a true *story* collection: it contains only fiction.

High school students grow wings, two boys embark on a road trip to steal from their estranged mother, a girl takes up residence in a boulder, a retired couple confronts the realities of aging, and a young man is hired to snuggle. These are just a few of the plots you will find in the following pages. Each of the ten stories in this volume is intensely and profoundly its own, and we're very proud to be sharing them with you. Thank you for supporting *The Masters Review* and the writers we publish.

Kim Winternheimer

Founding Editor

The Masters Review

The Masters Review, Volume IV
Stories Selected by Kevin Brockmeier
Edited by Kim Winternheimer and Sadye Teiser

Front cover: Dollarphoto Club
Design by Kim Winternheimer

Interior design by Kim Winternheimer

First printing.

ISBN: 978-0-9853407-3-5

Printed in the USA

Contents

Introduction

Sometimes it seems as if the stray components of my life—my reading, my writing, my teaching, my recollections, my conversations—conspire to present me with a hundred different models of narrative a year, offering up a new one every few days, like weather systems. The problem is that, again like weather systems, those models never linger for long before they are supplanted. Once they're gone, they're gone. When the sun shines, it's as if the rain has never fallen, and when the rain falls, it's as if the sun has never shone.

Anyway, the most recent such model introduced itself to me through Christian Bobin's short novel *The Lady in White*, about the biographical circumstances and meditative experiences of Emily Dickinson:

> What was "real" life? Father and daughter had two very different responses to the question. For the father, real life was horizontal: the train and telegraph were brought to Amherst, contracts were signed, men were connected to one another, and all of that, to the rhythm of their exchanges, caused wealth to grow. For the daughter, real life was vertical: a movement from the soul to the soul's master—for which there was no need of a railroad. Our only commerce is with the heavens, glowing above our heads and in the depths of our restraint. In such commerce there is nothing to be gained, only a heightened sensitivity to the dried blood of Christ on the breast of a robin, as well

as an understanding that grows ever sharper, and therefore ever more painful, of the behavior of other people.

A day comes when no one is a stranger to you anymore. This terrible day marks your entry into real life.

A good story, I think, offers both these visions of life simultaneously: the horizontal and the vertical. The horizontal line of a story runs through its plot, its mysteries, its moral dilemmas; the lessons its characters either learn or fail to; the relationships they nurture or injure, commence or dissolve; even the way the prose solves the puzzle of its own construction—which is to say, whatever it is that energizes a narrative toward its ending. Its vertical line can be found in those moments when a story stops to brace itself before the world, listening more closely than people ordinarily do, observing more carefully and embracing more intimately; those moments when through some seemingly accidental pattern of phrasing, music, sound, and intimation it offers up a sharp reminder of how it feels to be alive—which is to say, whatever it is that energizes a narrative toward the instant.

The horizontal aspect of a story is what keeps you turning its pages. The vertical aspect is what makes you pause over them.

As diverse as the ten selections in this edition of *The Masters Review* are, they have this in common: each of them is cut through by a vision of the world and its capacities, and also of narratives and *their* capacities, that is at once vertical and horizontal. That is what marks them to my eye as stories of such high accomplishment. They all made me feel, as I sat quietly before them, that I was participating more fully in my own experience, yet never once did their momentum suffer or their tension slacken as a result. All of them, moreover, are brimming with good prose: dynamic, exact, and inventive, keenly individuated and emotionally suggestive. Here are just a few of the pleasures awaiting you as you read on—a sentence apiece (or, in one case, a tight little sentence-cluster) from each of the stories in this volume:

- It was true that when Annabelle laughed, the sound was richer than any other laugh; when she looked sad, her eyes were deeper than anyone else's.

- The two trade bites from one another's plates, the girl, some kind of Millie or Jenny, togged up in civic softball white and blue.

- People, when they cared, did things like that, he thought; they made leaps and became themselves.

- Churchwomen tittered over him, continually blessing his heart, while he hunkered behind pews, peering over the seats with his wide milky eyes, which were like two full moons with inviolable craters for pupils.

- A girl is a porous compaction of subcutaneous layers.

- She inhabited the feeling gingerly, as if it were a tent she'd pitched without instructions. It was standing. It could fall.

- His mouth drew up, full of tannins, and he felt like he was chewing on aspirin and chalk, his tongue turning to fine sandpaper and rolling sideways out of his mouth like when you give a dog peanut butter, his cousins laughing at him.

- My Snuggle Summary Evaluation does not look promising.

- If we had only found each other, only discovered our connection, only fucked and loved and talked and comforted each other, only bared our hearts and bodies to each other, we might still be together.

- In that faraway cell, which nobody would ever find, I wrote: *I am safe here.*

If in those lines you can hear the attention, insight, receptivity, or humor of a singular verbal mind, and if you can sense those minds beginning to spin their fascinations, then you're bound to appreciate these stories as much as I do.

—Kevin Brockmeier

The Masters Review

ten stories

The Tenshi Project

Courtney Bird

Almost everyone agreed that the death of Rodrigo Bradley had been an accident. It wasn't like Rodrigo to leave his mother, forever, without a note. It wasn't like Rodrigo to wear turquoise gym shorts and a windbreaker on his last day (the gym shorts with a tear over the left hip, or was that from the fall?). It wasn't like him to pick somewhere quiet, somewhere in Brooklyn, if he intended to kill himself. Had Rodrigo intended to die, he would have done something flashier. The Empire State. The roof of his parents' apartment building on the Upper East Side. He would have worn a black suit, like Johnny Cash.

His obituary said things like captain of the basketball team, editor-in-chief of the literary magazine, straight-A student. It said that he liked to take the subway up to Fort Tryon Park and watch the sunset over the George Washington Bridge with his girl-friend Frances and that his favorite sunset had been on September 19, 2012, because of the way the raindrops, still clinging to the branches, refracted the light. Frances wrote the obituary. At his funeral, she read a sestina. Frances was a poet. She didn't mention his wings because wings are clichéd. Someone could pull it off, like Cummings or Rilke or Emily Dickinson—*Hope is the thing with feathers / that perches in the soul.* But we were only in high school and Frances said she wasn't famous enough to write about wings.

Someone photographed the body for the coroner before they peeled it from the road, before they cleaned the feathers and the blood from the hood of the taxi that had been parked outside the abandoned paper warehouse. The next day, the photograph was on the cover of the *Post*. Rodrigo was lying face down, with his wings splayed out all around him, the left one reaching toward the sidewalk, the right bent inward at an unnatural angle. The feathers were the burnt copper of a prairie hawk. The caption said *Icarus Grounded* and a lot of people found that offensive, like the newspaper had forgotten that he was just a normal kid with friends who would miss him. The photograph itself became instantly famous.

"He wasn't exactly the sharpest knife in the drawer. Like, street smarts," Molly said. "I mean, the bottle comes with a warning. There's like a whole information packet they send with the kit."

"How do you know?" I said. It had been two weeks since Rodrigo died. Frances hadn't come back to school and our teachers taught in the half dark, too disheartened to turn on the lights, or maybe afraid that the light would illuminate things they didn't want us to see: the bags under their eyes, the taut muscles behind their jaws. Molly wouldn't talk about anything but Rodrigo. His wings were too big for the coffin. His feathers were selling on eBay for $20.00 each.

Molly turned her back to me and glanced over her shoulder. "Notice anything?"

"Not really," I said. Molly was my girlfriend of maybe a month and she was always asking me to notice things. Her hair. Her shoes. Whether or not I thought her pearl earrings brought out the whites of her eyes.

She looked disappointed. "Oh well, you will."

"Wait," I said. "What does the warning say?"

"That the wings aren't for flying. Duh. I mean, look at Annabelle." She nodded toward Annabelle Stevens, who stood outside the English room down the hall. Her wings, a warm midnight black, swept the floor behind her. It was true that when Annabelle laughed, the sound was richer than any other laugh; when she looked sad, her eyes were deeper than anyone else's eyes. But maybe she had been that way before? I couldn't remember.

"So it's to make you prettier?" I said.

"It's not just about being pretty. They show you who you are inside. And they make you more yourself. Like Lena's wings? Kind of a color that isn't a color? And she's like that, you know. A hippie girl. She likes simple things. If she were a bird, she'd probably be a sparrow."

"How do you know sparrows like simple things?"

"Have you ever seen a sparrow?"

"I think so," I said.

*   *   *

That night, Molly called and told me to turn on Channel 356. I was lying on the living room floor with my homework spread out around me. My dad was on the couch in his flannel robe, earphones in. He had this new thing about listening to audio books because he said it hurt his eyes to look at a computer screen all day and then come home and look at more tiny letters. Now he was listening to something called "The Rise of the Third Reich," which meant that sometimes at dinner he'd talk about the difference between a good leader and a good person. He opened one eye when the phone rang and said, "Is it your girlfriend? Mary?"

I shook my head and mouthed the right name. *Molly.*

"356?" I said to her. "But this is a shopping network."

"Ben, what do you think my wings would look like?"

"I don't know," I said. "Like rusty kind of?"

"That's rude."

"A good rusty?"

I imagined her on the couch with her slippers on, her hair pulled back in a long French braid. Maybe laying on the floor just like me. Both of us watching the same commercial for tea tree oil shampoo.

"Just wait for it," she said. "It will come on again."

By the time it did, my dad was breathing that sleep rhythm and I could hear the slow whine of his book like white noise. The infomercial was in Japanese. Everything but the phone number at the bottom of the screen. It wasn't the typical thing—a woman with a painted-on face holding some earrings while an old guy in a suit said, "And look at the way the light bounces inside the diamond." Instead, there was a monastery with a red stone promenade and mountains popping up out of some mist. Then there was a stone room with two monks by the window, the old monk sitting on a stool with his back all hunched over and the young one painting along his shoulder blades. Then there were people with wings walking the streets of Tokyo. They wore suits. They stood on their roofs, watching traffic seventy stories below. They hung laundry. They climbed to the top of the dripping mountains. They knelt in the rice paddies, their wings folded on their backs, but stretching every few minutes. The children played hopscotch, the downy flakes from their feathers scattering on the pavement, their wings clawing up toward the sky.

At the end, it said in English, *Call for your starter kit today*. Is this what Rodrigo did? Watched the shopping channel in the middle of the night and called some 800 number? Did Frances tell him to? Did she know he was doing it? It wasn't like he was the first. I'd been seeing them everywhere: Central Park, the library, the subway platform, disappearing into a taxi, a hand reaching out to pull the feathers in.

"Jesus, they need a new marketing guy," my father said.

"Weren't you sleeping?" I said.

"I don't sleep, Ben. You know that."

He stood up, put the audio book player in the pocket of his robe. Then he said, "It does seem to be catching on, doesn't it? Every asshole wants to carry around twice his body weight. Worse than being pregnant."

*   *   *

The next day, *The New York Times* printed an op-ed celebrating the photograph of Rodrigo's body on the pavement. The writer called it a Pulitzer Prize contender, for the way it captured the plight of human existence. She called attention to the caves of shadow beneath every feather and the dark patch of blood above Rodrigo's right shoulder. She asked what the photographer had meant by the cross hanging from the rearview mirror of the cab, as if he'd put it there for the picture. She pointed out that the viewer could almost make out Rodrigo's face reflected in naked, impressionistic strokes on the cab door.

"Human existence?" Klaus Taylor said when it came up during math. "But it's so profoundly inhuman."

"Is it?" Mr. ten Holder was younger than the other teachers. He believed that math was the foundation of all knowledge. He often told us that his greatest fear was to die before someone mathematically reconciled the concepts of quantum mechanics and general relativity. "What does it mean to be human? I think the answer to that is constantly changing. Changing exponentially. How many people in this school alone are growing wings? How many people in the United States? In Japan? In the world?"

"Well, not the poor countries," Klaus said.

"So how expensive is it?" I said.

"Do you think wings make *me* less human?" Lena called from the back row, where she sat perfectly upright on a stool. Lena's hair was nearly to her waist. It ran over her shoulders and down her back between her wings, like water. Lena was the girl that every guy in school secretly loved; that every girl secretly envied. She was effortless. That day, she was wearing a dead daisy behind her ear.

"I don't know," Klaus said. "I'm not a biologist."

"I'm not talking about biology," Lena shot back. "Why are they different than the tattoo on your shoulder? Or Monica's nose job?"

"They're different," Klaus said.

*   *   *

When Frances came back to school, her feathers were tipped in blue. Sometimes, she wrapped them around herself and disappeared and no one asked about it. Over the next few weeks, other people stopped using backpacks. They cradled books in their arms or slung messenger bags over one shoulder; Ernest Penman carried his father's briefcase. I began to see the outline of a chrysalis underneath Molly's t-shirt, like the skin on her back had expanded and grown lumpy. She complained that her ankles were swollen and that her skin was extra sensitive. When I touched her chest, she pushed my hand away and said it hurt. When I kissed her, she said her lips hurt too. Everyone was changing. I don't know if it was about Rodrigo. Some people said that we were celebrating his life. But other people said that Rodrigo was a blip, that the world was heading inexorably in one direction and that it was our responsibility to move forward. They said that Rodrigo's death shouldn't slow us down. We were looking for what it meant to be human. To reach. To strive. To become our best selves. Wasn't that what we'd been doing for thousands of years? Today, the wings might not enable us to fly but fifty years from now? One hundred? What couldn't we do? Where couldn't we go? It was our duty to Rodrigo. Didn't Leonardo daVinci build shoes that could walk on water? Didn't he design flying machines?

"But it hurts," I said. "Why would you do something that hurts?"

And I said, "Isn't this why Rodrigo died?"

And Molly said, "Exactly. He's an inspiration."

They called the rest of us conservative and old-fashioned. They said we were scared. When their wings hatched, they clustered together and compared their colors. Molly still pushed me away, saying my lips hurt, my lips hurt. But then I saw her kissing Dylan Thompson on the sidewalk and their wings were curling in toward each other. They disappeared in a gazebo of feathers and I was left to eat lunch with Patty the Fatty and Lou, who had never kissed a girl at all. Sometimes I thought to myself, this is the breaking of a weak heart. And it appeared to me then that the wings made their wearers strong.

"How do we know it isn't simply evolution?" Mr. ten Holder said. "Is technology some evil force? Is it not a legitimate expression of life? How can we say, this is wrong or that is wrong? This is not a natural process because *we* created it? This *is* nature."

He unfurled his own massive wings, a deep brown like wet soil.

"I guess we're going to have to raise the ceilings in here," Klaus muttered. He looked diminished. Everyone else's wings rose around him like a forest at night. I wondered if I looked the way he looked. Smaller than the smallest tree. No leaves. Pale. Silver, almost. And everyone else flush with new life.

*   *   *

I called the 800 number at three in the morning. My parents weren't against it—on the contrary, my father had invested in the Tenshi Group, the Japanese lab that originated the formula—but it was embarrassing to want so desperately to change myself. To admit any kind of discontent in front of my parents was, I felt, like telling them that they had created an imperfect kid. I waited for thirty-seven minutes to speak with a representative. I almost hung up, but I kept thinking of Molly kissing Dylan Thompson and of Klaus and Patty the Fatty and of Frances, whose cheeks were red again and who now walked on her toes, as if her wings were drawing her upwards. And I thought of how the news anchors on NBC had begun reporting from outside the studio because their wings couldn't fit through the doors; and of the Pope, who said maybe this is the way of God; and Mr. ten Holder saying this is merely a return to what we are and weren't we familiar with the Hypostasis of the Archons or at the very least, the Gospel of Truth? No, we said. We are not.

The woman on the other end of the phone had a British accent. She sounded like she was sitting in an office, in a long row of other women paid to be chipper, with headsets on.

"We recommend two serums," she said. "The first for the hatching and the second for the healing. It's eucalyptus, so it feels nice. Cooling," she said. "It reduces swelling."

No one at school had mentioned swelling.

"Anything else I should be aware of?" I said. "Like side effects?"

"Not really," she said. "I mean, it's not FDA approved or however you say in the U.S., but that's only a matter of a time."

In History the next day, Frances told me I looked different. "At peace," she said. She'd started brushing her hair again, which we took as a good sign. Sometimes, she raised her hand in class and when she did, it seemed obvious that she was doing homework.

"I did it," I said. "I ordered the stuff. The wings."

"Oh, right! I got mine before—you know," she said. And then she said, "After it happened, I tried to cut them off. I blamed them for Rodrigo."

"Then why—?"

"What's the sense in blaming? Accidents happen. Think of how many people *haven't* died, for instance. And anyway, now I love them. It's like what Plato says. Before the gods got angry, we each had two sets of arms and two sets of legs. Two hearts. And then the gods chopped us in half and now we spend our whole lives trying to feel complete again." She looked down the hall, at wings crowding like lines of laundry, dancing, obscuring the people behind them. "I feel like I've found that other half and it's *inside* of me."

"How did Plato know?" I said. "How can you know?"

But she was right. It wasn't imagined; it was universal. We all felt abandoned. We all wanted to be a part of someone else. Molly holding Dylan's hand.

I walked around in a daze of anticipation. To feel whole!

*   *   *

The serums arrived on a Saturday morning. My parents were gone for the day, at some country retreat put on by the board of the Museum of Natural History. It wasn't a big deal. It wasn't like my parents were major donors. Not as major as Lena's, for instance.

In the small white box, underneath layers of brown paper, I found the vials. The liquid inside moved with the lethargy of jellyfish, dense and bubbling. The instruction manual was thicker than the manual for my contact solution, thinner than the manual for my cell phone. It said, side effects may include nausea and dry mouth. Avoid direct sunlight. Do not use while pregnant. Do not operate heavy machinery. Avoid sitting in hard-backed chairs, especially in the final days when the wings could hatch at any moment. It said, apply hatching serum for two weeks, at the same time every day for best results. Apply to the shoulder blades only. Application to feet or other body parts may result in deformity. The English text was in a tiny font on the verso of each page, a translation of the Japanese characters. It looked like an afterthought.

In the bathroom, I took off my shirt and dipped a Q-tip into the first serum. The liquid coalesced hungrily around the cotton bulb. I fingered the curve of my shoulder blade, watching my hand trawl my back in the mirror. This was the path that a wing should take. I double-checked the drawing in the manual.

*   *   *

Pain, my mother taught me, is produced by the brain. The body sends a message that says, "I am damaged," and the brain sends back a message that says, "This hurts. This needs to be fixed." The brain is not the same thing as your imagination, she said. Just as every square is a rectangle, but every rectangle is not a square.

*   *   *

I reapplied every night and every morning. Two long valleys appeared. Then hills pushing against my skin. On the fourth night, I couldn't sleep. I took out an old picture of my mother lying on the beach, her pregnant belly cradled in a hole my dad had dug to fit me, the baby. I'd seen the picture a thousand times: my mom turned toward the camera with her cheek resting in the sand, smiling as if the coolness of the sand was a relief.

I wondered if my mom felt back then like I felt now. If she was giddy all the time. If the joy hurt. If it electrified every single cell. And was Molly the same? Did she feel like a million sea monkeys had been let loose in her shoulder blades?

When I looked at myself in the mirror, I was surprised by my eyes. Had they always been so blue? Had there always been a brown freckle at the edge of my left iris?

The pain was localized in my back. I felt branches of something twining around my spinal cord, almost caressing it. I told myself, pain means it's working. By Wednesday, I couldn't fit my backpack over the ridges. My mother asked and I told her. She shook her head.

"I don't know what you want me to say," she said. "It's your body."

When I told my dad, he said, "I hear the molting process is a messy one. I hope you're ready."

I went to school and the hallways seemed to be flooded with golden light, as if the light from the fluorescents was richer now. Everyone smiled at me; we shared a secret that grew inside of us and we carried an energy that was for ourselves alone. Independent of the pavement and the steel buildings and the computers. And I was getting close. The skin on my back was stretched thin, nearly transparent. There was a darkness there beneath it.

*   *   *

It began on Thursday. The unraveling. Klaus didn't even notice when his skin split open until Lena saw the puddle behind his chair and screamed and then everyone was standing and backing away and Mr. ten Holder said, "Ben, please go get the nurse." Who had ever seen blood so black? The tiny talons were scratching to get out until finally the wings yawned out and up, with all of us watching and Klaus looking over his shoulder. There was nothing beautiful about them. They were bent and wet and paper-thin, like a gargoyle's wings if gargoyles weren't made out of stone. The skin was traced with the hideous mapping of raised veins. The top wing twitched involuntarily.

I felt a tug in my back and realized with horror that soon it would be happening to me. Maybe not right now. Maybe not tomorrow. But it would be happening. Still, it was true that everyone else's wings had feathers and they were beautiful and strong. It was true that we were happy in our beauty and our strength. It was true that the wings revealed us and I had nothing to hide.

"What is beauty?" Mr. ten Holder said, once the mess had been wiped up and Klaus had been taken, crying, to the nurse's office. "Why did we shrink at the sight of Klaus's wings? Isn't it arbitrary?"

"Beauty is a natural condition of the brain," Annabelle said. "Social constructs of beauty only exist because we're instinctively drawn to beauty."

Mr. ten Holder was pale. "Klaus has different wings. So what? It's superficial."

"But the wings tell us who we are," Annabelle said. "The serum is supposed to interact with your genes."

I wasn't like Klaus. Or like Veronica Wagonseller, whose back was covered in one hundred and eighty seven pairs of tiny wings. Someone said it was because she slept around, but I couldn't remember whether that was true. My genes were pure.

"It's not the serum," Lewis Anderson said. "It's something to do with Klaus."

"It's a new technology," Mr. ten Holder said. He was sweating. "There are bound to be accidents."

"Rodrigo's wings were beautiful," Lena said.

*   *   *

There was no pain for me. I woke up in my bed, warm and sticky with blood. They moved against the sheets and I felt the muscles in my back spasm, a nausea bloom in my stomach, then the slow sensation that I'd given birth to something alien, with its own beating heart and its own mind hunkering down into the cracks of my vertebrae. It felt parasitic. Uncontrollable. Hungry. When I stood, I almost fell backwards with the weight of them. When I ate breakfast, I felt them leaching my nutrients.

*   *   *

It was just like anyone else's hatching. Everyone at school touched my feathers and said how beautiful, how soft! They offered me tips on products—this one will make the feathers shinier, this one will make them fluffy. Molly baked me cookies. Said I looked handsome.

When Klaus came back, his arms were thinner, his face grayer. He would sit on the front steps at lunch with a cape cast over himself, reading his comic books. I was afraid of him at first, but they say misery loves company.

"Even if it were my genes," Klaus said. "I don't have any control over them."

"I know," I said.

We were sitting on the steps. My wings were all around me and I was warm. But still, everything ached, like a homesickness in my bones.

"Do you ever get the feeling that they want something?" I said. "Like they have a mind of their own?"

He looked at a page in his comic book but I could tell he wasn't reading it. Then he slammed it shut and said, "It makes me nauseous to think about it."

Eventually his wings got so heavy he couldn't leave his bed and his mother had to sponge-bathe them to keep the skin from rotting. I brought him comic books every Sunday. We didn't talk about the wings anymore. We did our best to pretend they didn't exist.

*   *   *

Klaus gave me a sealed envelope, something he'd asked me to put at Rodrigo's grave, but I didn't know where the graveyard was so I climbed to the top of the paper warehouse where he had died. My body felt unbearably heavy and by the fifth floor I regretted the whole thing but I couldn't turn around. How had Rodrigo managed to fit inside this stairwell? I hadn't learned to fold my wings up small. Hadn't learned how to connect the instructions in my brain to the tendons in my back. Or to control the things they wanted. Avocados. Street hot dogs. Cilantro. Their feathers scraped the brick walls, no way to go back. This was claustrophobia. This was a panic attack.

From the roof, I could see the Brooklyn Bridge straddling the river. The waves tossed the afternoon light. It was November. I felt the cold on the raised skin of my back, the place where my mother had cut slits in my shirts and sweaters to fit the wings. She'd cried when I showed them to her and said, "My beautiful baby."

There was a heaviness that came with being whole. No one let on about that. No one said that maybe the gods were right to take our other arms, our other legs. That maybe wholeness wasn't something that should come from inside. That maybe fallen angels weren't meant to rise again, but only to fall and fall. That maybe falling was not such a bad thing. Mr. ten Holder had stopped coming to school. People said he was getting divorced, was sick, was dead, had moved to Africa, had moved to Russia, had cut his wings off with a kitchen knife and nearly bled to death on the linoleum floor. If anyone knew the truth, it wasn't us.

I leaned out over the railing. It looked just like the infomercial. I could barely make out the people down on the sidewalk, only feathers and feathers and feathers. I held the envelope up to the light and traced Rodrigo's name with my finger. Then I pulled my arm back and threw the thing as far into the sky as I could.

It wove back and forth on currents of air, eventually disappearing, eventually landing. Picked up by some stranger. Read. And I stood there in my sneakers watching it fall. No windbreaker. The alien parts of me yearning to try it, just this once, to be free and whole, and why not? There was the air and the sun so very far away, the light on the windows, the river glistening on the horizon.

Someday Soon, You'll Be On Fire

Sarah Smith

Gordon is a man of great sensitivity and wishes to become a monk. He packs a suitcase with what he thinks he will need for this endeavor: white t-shirts, the newest of his underwear, thick socks, and a photograph of his mother laughing prettily in the backyard, framed by chain-link diamonds. He takes a bus to the monastery with the most pleasing name: the Poor Clares of Perpetual Adoration in Cleveland, Ohio.

He arrives in early evening, and after knocking a few times and standing there in mortification, simply opens the door and goes in. Three monks in cassocks the color of raisins are clearing away dishes from the long dinner table in silence. The monk who greets him points to his own closed lips while smiling and nodding to indicate that they are within an interval of no speech. Gordon nods in understanding and is led to a stone-walled room with a bed, a cross, and a nightstand bearing the Bible. Gordon puts on his thick socks and arranges the photograph of his mother on the nightstand. The nightstand is too small to hold both the Bible and the photograph, so he sits at the edge of the bed holding the Bible in his lap.

After ten minutes of Gordon attending to the high-pitched whine of blood in his ears, a different monk arrives with a hot-water bottle. This monk turns out the light as he exits, leaving Gordon to find the lip of the covers by feel. He slides into the bed as if trying not to disturb a glass of water balanced on its opposite edge. The Bible he places under his pillow. He has never been given a hot-water bottle before, and so hugs it to his chest and falls asleep.

*   *   *

He wakes to the sound of monks moving along the halls, dresses himself quickly, and follows the others to the long table for breakfast. They pass a crock of porridge. Every time Gordon's spoon clangs against the bottom of his bowl, his nerves leap and he chides himself for doing things too clumsily. The rest of them eat soundlessly, like statues feeding on air.

A monk from the far edge of the table rises and walks to a low shelf under a massive oil painting of a monk. He strikes a wooden chime, and the monks begin to relax, grumbling, testing out their unused voices. No one wants to be the first to speak, although they shift and adjust themselves, clearing their throats with thick hisses.

The monk who struck the chime approaches Gordon and places a hand on his shoulder.

"Son, we welcome you. What have you brought to trade?"

"Pardon my ignorance," Gordon says, "but I did not know I should bring anything to barter."

"Ah, yes," says the monk, "but the most wealthy are often the least aware of their riches."

"I am a man of great sensitivity," he says. "I have brought very little, for I am not in thrall to the material world."

Gordon expects a benevolent wash of head nodding to greet his statement, but there are a few disgruntled (though muffled) sighs.

"Come, let us see what you have brought. I'm sure your modesty is misleading."

The monk in charge leads the rest of them to the room. Gordon takes out the suitcase, opens it on the bed, and lays out his t-shirts and socks. At the last moment, he adds the framed photograph of his mother to the offering.

The lead monk frowns at the meager collection. "I believe I saw a few more items in the suitcase there," he says.

"Those are my personal underwear," Gordon says. "They are not new."

"They look newish."

"It is a personal garment."

"Please."

Gordon adds his underwear to the offering. The monks line up in some sort of predetermined order and parade past the items. They form a huddle to discuss the display; some of the monks make exasperated hand gestures. The lead monk emerges to announce that they will take the underwear.

"I'm afraid I don't understand," says Gordon.

"In exchange for the underwear, we will give you one night's lodgings."

"But I've already stayed the night."

"This is precisely why we must now ask you to leave."

"I am a man of great sensitivity. I wish to join your order."

"The only way to join our order is to stay eighty nights in our company and absorb our teachings."

Gordon is stunned. The other monks pack his suitcase for him and gather the now-cold water bottle. They usher him back through the hallway and leave him on the front step before he has altogether gotten his bearings. As they file back into the monastery, one monk straggles behind and shakes Gordon's hand warmly, palming a note.

The note says: "We really like cheese."

*   *   *

Gordon returns to his apartment late—having no return bus ticket, he had to wait three hours merely to board a bus bound even in the general direction of Erie, and while waiting read abandoned newspapers and the first two-thirds of a child's chapter book in which two girls become witches or, through their particular and ritual-driven method of play at becoming witches, merely become best friends. Though it was confusing, the story managed the feat of comforting Gordon, as it insisted that the very brave and humble among us, and we all think of ourselves as such, secretly, are capable of magical acts, which is why he concealed the book in his duffel bag even after the girl it belonged to returned to the waiting area, looking under the modular benches and twice in the ladies' room while her frazzle-headed mom hung out the door of the bus waiting specially to depart.

The refrigerator in his apartment is empty except for condiments and a red cabbage gone soft on one end like a deflating basketball, and the bed covers are packed away in a vacuum-sealed bag in the hall closet. He had prepaid three months' rent and left a letter on the table directing his landlady to sell the rest of his things in case he chose simply to default on the lease by staying indefinitely, plus a fifty dollar bill for her trouble in clearing the place. Next to the refrigerator, a nest of dead vodka bottles like a city of all skyscrapers. Gordon winces. He had not planned on seeing them again. In order to stay the night, he has to undo the preparations he had enacted to keep the place free of rust, dust, and pests, the very general thought of which reminds him that he hasn't eaten since two packets of peanuts that morning.

At the Chinese restaurant on the corner, he orders his usual: a dozen crab Rangoons and a side of white rice. Milky jade buddhas have been taped to the pull strings on the overhead fans, joggling slightly as the air disturbs them. A flutter of movement pulls his eyes up from the real estate circular he is reading on the bench near the door: Maryanne Phillips is seated under a red fan, eating with her fifteen-year-old daughter. The two trade bites from one another's plates, the girl, some kind of Millie or Jenny, togged up in civic softball white and blue.

"Gordon! We thought you were on some kind of sabbatical already," Maryanne says, having sensed his lingering glance just before he shifted it to the fish tank by the register.

"Well. I'm still making my preparations, as it were."

"No kidding. Three months, that's a real chunk. Where are you off to, again?"

"A stretch of farm work at my uncle's in Missouri. There's so much alfalfa this year it's like, blooming in the fields before they can get to it, which is bad, I guess, but my uncle's getting kind of up there in years."

"Well that should be quite the change for you. You'll be a rough-neck by the end of the summer."

"Ha, right." He hadn't considered this flaw in his planned cover story, the mechanics of which were designed to be plausible and slightly sentimental. Some further backup plan will be necessary if the planned transition to monk life falls through—he imagines swinging hammers with their handles wrapped in sandpaper to achieve the right calluses, a thought made all the more dreadful by the mysterious and utter failure of his first visit to the monastery.

"Do you work for my mom?" asks Millie or Jenny, swinging her legs in such a forceful tic that it bounces her from side to side, a kinetic gesture similar to the joggling statuettes attached to the ceiling fans' pull cords. The recombinant effects of these motions occurring within the same chunk of vista available to Gordon's eyesight make for a visual unsteadiness, and he feels he must suddenly lean forward a bit to keep from falling over.

"Yes," he says, "she's my boss."

"Oh, Gordon, sheesh. No, honey, we work on the same team, but I'm the senior member, not the boss."

"Whatever. Do you want my water chestnuts?" Millie/Jenny asks.

"Sure, sweetie, just put them at the edge of my plate. I swear, sometimes I feel like I'm half mom, half garbage disposal." Maryanne, most of the time, reacts with self-effacing aw-shucksisms meant to defray her implacable all-the-time competence, not only as a standardized test copyeditor but also as a mom, taxpayer, and, Gordon is sure, doggedly pleasant person to be seated next to in an airplane. She wearies him beyond all possible sense.

A takeout bag appears on the counter, and Gordon uses it to make his hasty exit, pacing back up the street in swirling midsummer winds. He arranges himself on the floor in front of the television, refusing to tuck into his Rangoons until he's found a program to watch. He ends up on an extended advertisement for a masticating juicer disguised thinly as a cooking show. A redheaded woman feeds carrots into the machine and delivers a monologue on colon health, all without breaking eye contact with the camera. Gordon imagines her leaving the sound stage, her television makeup a garish mask in the soft LA twilight, and picking up a dozen crab Rangoons from some strip mall. This makes her much more appealing. He gets his coat and walks to the liquor store just before it closes. They still know his face, but not his name. The infomercial has gone off the air by the time he gets back, replaced by cop shows. The second person they interview is always, always guilty.

*   *   *

Gordon *is* a man of great sensitivity, and as such saw the obliteration of his personal sovereignty as a crucial first step in acclimation to monk life. Indeed, he began dissociative prep work the moment he left his workplace for the last time, repeating cut-rate mantras he found on a website maintained by some order of Rosicrucian monks who nevertheless had learned a fair amount about Adobe Flash. This should have made him at least marginally suspicious, but, well, desperation. He is sitting in a bar called Paradise for Travelers. It is paradise for travelers. They bring him the glasses and bottles he asks for. They bring him pink pickled eggs once he has been there a long time.

Sensitivity is not useful, he thinks. It is selfish and shallow, calibrated only to one set of appetites and disappointments. He could probably obtain whatever enlightenment he chooses at the public library, a horrible and exhausting thing to know. Why not volunteer at a food pantry or read bedtime stories to abused children in a group home? He could make himself useful, but prefers a solution in which the labor of discipline requires only one vast gesture, a gesture irreversible and inert, a little like dieters who would rather enroll in fat camp than face the totality of personal responsibility to be exercised daily, at every location, and with horrifying ubiquity.

Somebody plays bad jazz on the jukebox. Fat slashes of sun sneak in through the blinds. There is something about this time of day that flattens him. The hot, sort of dazed feeling he remembers from childhood after eating too many cookies, a thick and panicky mien in which his thoughts would stay on the searing, gilded fact of whatever he happened to look at, which usually occurred for some reason on rainy days, and which it seemed could never be accurately described to anyone, family or no, who seemed to lumber around to the television and watch whatever news appeared there with no anxiety or displacement. A blue windbreaker on a jogger. The beveled glass handles of knives in a display window downtown, a white porcelain bear from a box of tea left on its side under the couch, never able to right itself. Once, he asked his father for a ride to Bible camp during summer vacation, and his father spiked his plastic juice glass into the sink with so much force that it shattered, was thrown away, and never spoken about again. The way fields in summer are hotter than the sidewalk, nauseating heat conducting through sneaker soles. Killing whole days as a child pressing in on his belly button to feel a queasy jolt. Lament, lament. This is the standard affect. The very most common way to feel.

*   *   *

Gordon prepares more carefully for his second trip to the monastery. For all his attempted research, he finds nothing detailing the initiation rites of the Poor Clares, although he does discover that Bereft Clares are almost always an order of nuns, not monks. Also, there is the problem of deciding what offerings they might accept as payment for a night's lodgings. He could bring more underwear, certainly, but the contents of his austere duffel gave him few context clues to work from, and in his preparatory, dissociative zeal, he had already given away or sold the most barterable of his possessions.

So to prepare, he trawls the thrift stores of Erie, first for a second duffel, and secondarily for items to fill it which would permit him to stay at the monastery long enough. He no longer thinks of "long enough" as the interval required to become a monk, but long enough to figure out what goes on there. Evaluating objects for their monk-captivating capacities, he regresses into a childhood game he had played with various catalogs. He would flip through them, settling on items that seemed to project from themselves a fully realized portrait of a life that was not his: a small, monogrammed telescope to affix to a desk, flanked by woodgrain ballpoint pens capped by the slender, golden cones that also held them to the placard; globes that opened into a brandy set with snifter and goblets; stacking, rudimentary ladders to be installed next to the second-floor windows in case of a fire. Not that the objects in the PickSaver exhibit the same aspirational Old World aesthetic of those catalogs (not ordered by anyone in his family, but addressed always to "current resident"). They give off an aura of tedium, instead: crocheted cozies for margarine tubs disguised under the skirts of a doll and doorstoppers made by repetitive, geometric folding of the phone book.

For a second time, Gordon boards a bus to Cleveland, this time with two duffel bags and a lunch sack of the finest cheeses on offer at Kraynick's Deli. He enters without his former hesitation, and again, a monk shushes him to demonstrate an interval of silence. If they remember him from a week ago, none of the monks let on in the slightest.

Again, he unpacks in the austere room and accepts the hot-water bottle, but this time he can't sleep for wondering how the brothers will receive his offering. And he brought all his underwear, just as a kind of contingency measure. The whole haul, he reckons, merits at least a week's stay. Anticipating its evaluation, he lays it all out on his bed before he is even summoned to breakfast.

At breakfast, after the signal to commence talking, the same monk says again: "Son, we welcome you. What have you brought to trade?"

"Many things. They are on display in the room you so graciously offered me last night."

"Excellent," says the head monk, this time without the backdrop of grumbling.

He follows the monks into his room, where they file past the objects, a collection of devotional items, lacquered Bible verses rendered on woodgrain, and many pale Jesuses, their ribs showing, their facial hair retro, their eyes pulled upward in plaint. And the cheeses, of course.

After huddling up again to discuss the offering, the head monk approaches, a sad, faux-diffident smile puckering around his eyes.

"Son, I'm afraid none of this is quite right."

"But I brought underwear. And cheese."

"Cheese is a decadence. And as for underwear—well, it is a personal garment, you see."

"But you took my underwear last time."

"Did we?" He looks back to the huddle, each member of which shakes his head in puzzlement. "No, son, I think you must be mistaken."

"But I—"

"And as you have stolen a night's lodgings from us, we must ask that you not return until you bring sufficient materials to trade."

"Brother, I will, if only you'll tell me what items would be considered appropriate."

"What is appropriate? That question haunts us all, I assure you. If any of the men here knew what was appropriate, they would certainly offer their services elsewhere, and in other capacities." One monk, a great big beefeater, giggles and chews on a toothpick. The others fold around him. One dummy-slaps the back of his head.

The main monk looks a little like a faded country western star, deep parentheses framing either side of his mouth, with the facial leathering of men who have storied histories of drinking and smoking. His voice, though, is the meandering basso profundo of call-in radio advice programs, a fact Gordon did not notice during his previous visit. None of the monks try to pass him a note as he leaves this time. Gordon walks halfway down the block, then turns and walks back. The monk with the toothpick is sweeping the front steps, whistling an innocuous tune.

*   *   *

Maryanne has been setting her hair on fire. Not all of it at once, just a strand here or there that already looked split or dead. She waits for her husband and Tillie to go to sleep, feigning take-home work and sitting in the little pool of yellow light with the TV going until they are dead bored by the scene. She waits for them to actually both be asleep before going to the bathroom, opening the pebbled glass window, and fishing out the lighter, which, ironically, she stole from Tillie. Well, not stole, necessarily; she found it in one of her daughter's pockets during a pre-laundry search for pens and gum, and executed a seizure perfectly in line with her role as parental lawmaker, which act Tillie cannot appeal without incriminating herself, so.

Hairs burn a little like a fuse, leaving behind a powdery orange trail that dissolves into nothing when rubbed between the fingers, ending in a kinked little hook which she trims away with curved manicure scissors. The habit emerged out of plain air when Maryanne found the lighter. It just occurred to her as what she was going to do, although she also knew how pathetic it was as a coping mechanism. How even as self-immolation the act was callow and tame, lacking the enormity of a real gesture.

On this night, one of the networks is broadcasting Olympic gymnastics, engrossing to her daughter and husband, who follow along, predicting scores from the judging panel, which always contains, as a matter of ritual, one grossly unfair Russian. She looks over the same folder of standardized-test questions she's been using as a ruse for late working since the habit began. Nothing is wrong with any of them from a copyediting point of view, although Gordon Sortie's questions are uniformly strange. For example: "In James Baldwin's *Another Country*, what is the other country? A. Paris B. New York C. France D. Europe." For another example: "Macbeth is motivated by A. Lady Macbeth B. Greed C. Cowardice D. Shakespeare." As group leader, she is tasked with copyediting, not content monitoring, and so the clear impossibility of these questions appearing on any standardized test is strictly not her problem. All content produced by her team is forwarded to Harrisburg for analysis along a series of metrics. She can only imagine what effect Gordon's questions have at headquarters, where the sensitivity trainings are legend. He is one of those kids who might actually just have a very opaque sense of humor, she thinks, although he creeps her out too much to investigate.

By eleven p.m., her family is still glued to the set. Their lax summer bedtime hours for Tillie were invoked as a demonstration of trust, i.e. we're not just parental-enforcers, kiddo, and learning to spend your time productively involves letting go of some of this socially scripted authority, right? Which it would be hypocritical to revoke, especially in a scene of such rare teenage-daughter-and-dad unity. These are the moments of teen parenting she has been cautioned to grab the ass of and not let go, rare as they will increasingly be. Which makes Maryanne's inability to stop wishing them to bed so she can light the fuses of her hair one after another for who knows how long—one night she stayed up until dawn—feel especially monstrous and shitty.

"I'm going to take a bath," Maryanne announces.

"It's late," says her husband.

"I know. I just, looking at these things has me fried."

"You're working way too hard, mom."

"Ah, I know, sweetie. Maybe we can go see a movie tomorrow?"

"Mo-om, tomorrow's the floor routines."

"Tills loves the floor routines the most," her husband explains, now a loyal member of the gymnastics fan club.

"Oh, that's right. Well, maybe we can see a movie after the damn Olympics." Maryanne leaves them in the wake of her displeasure without looking back.

The tub takes a long time to fill, and Maryanne promises herself that she'll only permit the snick snick of the lighter—why does it always, always take two tries to produce a flame?—while the faucet's turned full-blast. Sitting around the corner on the lip of the toilet, she enters the weird reverie of watching the flame snap at the strand of hair, its burn traveling at some advanced rate, as if the rest of her time is spent trudging through something prerecorded and slowed for play-by-play analysis. She has been missing errors at work. Last week, a junior editor caught the phrases "pubic access television" and "left at the alter" in copy she had signed off on for preflight. Within the hour, it would have been printed up in the newsprint booklets of a grade ten reading comprehension battery; they only had the new guy read over it as a kind of training procedure. A monsoon of shit rains down upon whoever lets such errors through. Even though the copy was corrected in time, Maryanne goes cold in the temples just glossing over the memory. By the time she thinks to check on the water, the meniscus is pulsing just above the edge of the tub, one minute atmospheric adjustment away from spilling over. She slams the water off and grabs the juice glass still left there at the edge from bathing Tillie as an infant, when she used to sluice the shampoo out of her hair by cupping a palm around her forehead. It is a gesture Maryanne thinks everybody should be allowed to perform.

It takes her ten minutes to dump enough water down the sink, cup by cup, so she can finally sit in it, by which point the water is chillish.

"Mom, are you OK?" Tillie is leaning against the doorjamb on her way to bed.

"I'm just taking a bath, sweetie."

"We can see a movie tomorrow. It would be fun."

"Whatever you want, Tillie. It's fine."

"Can I come in and brush my teeth?"

"No, sweetie, just go to bed." Maryanne looks over the pale, bald islands her knees and breasts make in the water. She lowers one knee incrementally into the tub, and has a vision. Maryanne sees the islanders clambering for higher ground, rushing provisions to the missionary church on the highest hill with its one temple bell in retreat from the paranoiac tide that rises without stopping, the monkeys fighting for purchase in the upper layers of the canopy. "You'd better run," she says to them. "You guys are fucked."

*   *   *

So Gordon goes home to his ratbox apartment and takes the sheets from their vacuum-packed storage bag again. Defeat is complex, but it is not grief. There is no timetable for appropriate emotional responses, just one tall, nasty step to get down from. Gordon makes his bed and plumps the pillows and it looks good so he gets right in with his Rangoons and the chapter book about witch friends. But he is restless. His heart heaps around in his chest. He buys two bottles of vodka, and also a sleeve of red plastic cups, so the liquor store employees will think he is having a party.

*   *   *

"Occasionally a guy would take it too far. The job order says collect two large from some college girl dealing infinitesimal amounts of stepped-on product to her friends: bunnies, deer, and other woodland creatures. But a guy would want to get creative, would start thinking. And so rather than knock on her door and say, 'Hi, sweetie, I need the two large, please and thank you, mind if I sit while I wait? Yes, I'd love a cup of coffee,' he maybe starts hanging around her house costumed as a homeless figure standing asleep over a shopping cart freighted with human trash, sad shit, odds and ends from the drive-thru across the street. Just standing there, seemingly asleep even in the blaze of summer, occasional visits from patrolmen establishing him as a mentally void but undangerous nuisance. And he hangs out there so often that the girl's creepy part-Lebanese neighbor, who has a new girlfriend every week and takes online classes about film editing—not what you'd call a character of impressive rectitude—starts referring to him as 'the Oracle.' As in 'Hey, throw another steak on the grill for the Oracle' or just 'Anybody seen the Oracle today? Is he missing? Or is he *right behind you?* And our guy will keep this shit up for weeks just to establish a pattern, at which point I might remind you the original job order is massively fucking overdue, so now the girl owes ten large, which her idiot boyfriend tries to capitalize on by taking it to a casino, claiming to be just Dickie Doodles at counting cards. And just guess what happens there. And he doesn't tell her he lost all the money, but scrambles to make it back, cutting into side business, not like that's automatically bad, but a thing done with desperation, you know. And so the Oracle starts moving his cart gradually closer to her house, spooking the fuck out of her bunny and doe friends, but the girl is by this point inured to the whole business, sees it as a form of taxation for living in an interesting part of town. So she doesn't feel the panic until the Oracle, whose real name is Jed or Freddy or Marco, obviously, is on her front porch one day, and even then she kind of just deals with it by having the part-Lebanese neighbor come over more often to watch basketball. And now it's showtime: Our guy picks the lock and sedates the dog with drugged meat and just waits there for her to get home from class—marketing, clearly—and just jumps on her with such unnecessary zeal that she stumbles backward and hits her head on the marble coffee table. Well, hey, all of that is just supremely unnecessary. And where's the two large? Where's the ten large? From an operational point of view, it's as inefficient as looking for gold teeth in cat turds.

"So for these guys, they get put on chill-the-fuck-out retainer. You'd be amazed—amazed—how many guys get like this, just impossible at doing the normal routine, citing unused aptitudes and how as kids they were the porpoise in the school play and have never since experienced such wholesome elation. Like a 'we all have a truth' kind of thing. And don't pretend that substance abuse issues are not often bound up in the whole problem, which for the sake of their clarity and societal operation it is good to get them away from the mess to live cleaned up. We put them up in a nice little tucked-away institution up by the lake, call them the Poor Clares of Something, dress them up as monks, put them on daily observations of silence until they either chill the fuck out or, what happens more often, get so theatrical and demented, reading biographies of Rasputin and letting their thoughts get all mouth-breathingly cluttered that they're actually more useful as deputies and can be shipped anywhere in the country to take on the big hasslers who actually need and deserve the treatment they, in their operatic and blood-lusting hearts, are apt to dish out. And then, really, a whole other set of them never want to leave."

*   *   *

Dwight B., so called not due to it being his real name but rather because he resembles the profile of Dwight Eisenhower on the dollar, helps Dwight G. launder the robes, which is the most hellish chore. The monks, especially the newest ones, have lapsed, hygiene-wise, into the territory of dog stink in their work for Ames Iverson, which is usually collections-based. Laundry duty is a punishment, although according to official patter, all tasks are equal and assigned randomly. Dwight B. has no idea how Paterfamilias found out about the note he passed to the rube with the underwear, and really, who would not welcome a few reeking ounces of camembert to add some life to unending meals of lentils, he would like to know.

Dwight G., so called because it is his real name, although he went by Ratsnake among his colleagues, having always considered Dwight an embarrassing and geeky name, shakes out a robe over a trash can, and out tumble twelve or so soggy, gummed toothpicks. Brother Sibelius has been denied his cheroots, seeking to replace them first with lollipops and now this. Monkhood is also de facto rehab, something the Pater kind of enforces without seeming to do so in any tangible way. It's not like laundry is so hard. It's the shit you find in the pockets: a foxed-edged picture of a woman with bosoms like a shelf and a face like a hatchet, a little nugget of porridge crusted over but still squishy inside, your own personal comb which you had assumed (correctly) to be stolen a few weeks ago. And no less horrifying are the wear patterns on the robes themselves, hitched up around meaty asses in frequent sitting, or just put it this way, it's not hard to tell who touches his business often. They are a weak and terrified multitude. Dwight G. finds it difficult to meet others' eyes after a day in the laundry room, although in Dwight B. it engenders a tenderness which makes it difficult for the others to meet his eyes.

The Pater disturbs them, appearing in the doorway like a sudden gong. "Hey guys, stop it with the laundry for a minute."

They look up puzzled. Dwight B. is examining a length of braided broom straw almost long enough to be a bracelet which he was just about sneak into his pocket.

"You can talk. OK, OK, 'Brothers, I release you from your observation of silence.'"

"We're nowhere close to done, boss," says Dwight G.

"That's fine. I'm calling a meeting. We got a pilgrim out front."

"Another one?" asks Dwight B.

"The same one, actually." The Pater inclines his head and steeples his fingers. "At least I think so. He looks a little rougher, but I think it's the initial guy."

"Poor guy," says Dwight B.

"That poor guy is an asshole," says Dwight G. "Remember that stuff last time? And what the hell with the cheese?"

The rest of the brothers are already assembled around the dining table. Unsupervised talk is rare, and thus causes a certain snow day elation. Brother Sibelius and Brother Roy throw dice, which the Pater pockets, clucking his tongue. Previous policy on pilgrims has been to deny them outright if they're ladies; with men, the Pater likes to let them in and improvise an excuse to eighty-six them, strictly for his own entertainment. It says much about the Cleveland metro area's appetite for faith that, aside from Gordon, repeat pilgrimages have happened a total of never.

The trouble here is that clearly Gordon is in need and deteriorating rapidly. He now looks like somebody too acquainted with the sandwiches at bus stops, somebody whose private library of smells was condensed into one vast, epic volume with subplots and princesses and long, pointless episodes in the garden before dinner. That the actual purpose of the monastery verges away from the idea of offering helpful intervals, maybe just prayer, whatever good it is, seems moot to the Pater, watching this actual human actually suffering.

Brother Asher picks his teeth with a scratch-off ticket. Brother Van Loon asks the time and temperature; no one knows or answers. Brother Sibelius scratches "Debra, Debra, you cunt, you cunt" in the table. These men are not well; the Pater knows this. Over the shoulder of Dwight G. née Ratsnake, who flicks the back of his right earlobe with his yellowed middle finger, seemingly unaware of this tic, the Pater watches the young man sitting next to and nearly under a forsythia bush, mushing his eyes with the heels of his hands. This is a posture adopted in fatigue, a way to forestall headaches or eye tension, but to the Paterfamilias it always looks like utter self-abasement, the gesture of a child who has lost his mother or a con man who knows that whatever ruse he'd been stringing along was fucked, fucked, beyond fucked in the ass.

*   *   *

Maryanne understands the notion that displacement is a not especially healthy coping technique. Psychological trouble should be dragged out from under its rock and made to bear the awful light automatically; it only gets muscles if you let it stay under the surface. Suppressing her initial compulsion to set her hair on fire strand by strand, though, has led her to take longer baths, embroidering her interior tale of the islanders on her knee panicking, clambering for the high ground of the monastery.

It goes like this: The monastery is tasked to take care of a large, cylindrical bell. The bell is made of polished wood and sits suspended by strips of cloth at five points along its length, like a canoe. Unlike most bells of its size, it responds most notably to subtle gestures and tiny strokes. When struck by a mallet, it is only as loud as a speaking voice. But when a cricket lands on it, the bell rings out throughout the island, which is a nuisance on an island already so noisy with monkeys and children and husbands and radios and dice. To dampen those sounds, the monks practice a bell meditation in which they take turns striking the bell with a mallet. They only cease their observance in the case of a wedding or a funeral. Though wild, the bell sounds appropriately joyous or mournful on those occasions and only those occasions. At any other time, its zeal is disorienting. After even a brief episode of its unexpected ringing, the people in town below complain of unwell goats and mean-spirited comments from loved ones.

The first waves of refugees do little to upset the present system, and the monks are pleased to be of service in a fashion more literal than their general prayers. But steadily the waters rise—they're all fucked, after all, as Maryanne continues the saga—and soon villagers must be housed on the temple steps, and eventually on the platform which holds the bell. The occasional cricket is one thing, but the nudgings of children and sisters engaged in gestural conversation and two young lovers trying to scoot through to the farther part of the platform upset the bell often, which of course makes everyone edgier. And worse, the waters continue to rise. Everyone who can't fashion a raft is stranded on the temple roof, but still one monk must remain to strike the bell. It is most unfortunate, but of course lapping waves are even more gentle and plentiful than a flotilla of grasshoppers. And unlike grasshoppers, the waves aren't frightened away by the bell's vibrations. Now a monk must embrace the bell as if making love to it in order to tamp down its music. Very soon, the water will rise to the very height of the world and the bell will float free from the strips of cloth it rests on. And at that point it will be necessary to make a decision: to let the bell go on its own, clanging in the ripples to spread madness? Or to assign a monk to embrace it in a horribly undignified manner, possibly until he dies? What will they do?

Tillie stands on the other side of the door, listening to her mother occasionally adjusting the temperature by turning on the hot faucet with her toes. Tillie is aware that she is the one who's supposed to sulk in the tub. The opacity of someone more engaged with her interior world than sensible tasks should be hers, as it is ever the province of teenagers. Since the baths started, her mother has floated through the house, her hair always a little damp at the nape of her neck, waiting in amusement for her husband and daughter to step aside. Up from the basement come her records. On each cover, a po-faced, long-haired man stands moodily in a fen, occasionally with a banjo slung across his gut. She wears one loose purple dress. She won't do the dishes. She only eats potato chips and pop. She looks—it is horrible to say so—more beautiful than ever.

Because Maryanne is the house disciplinarian, though, her lassitude becomes something of a boon for Tillie. Sneaking out at night was never possible with her mother suggesting bracing rounds of Boggle from the couch where she would wait, hawkish, for Tillie to go up the stairs. And so now, Tillie has made her place in the vaulted company of Kimmie Cornwallis-Steiner, softball captain, giver of covert party suckjobs, defiant owner of a tweaking habit which will eventually land her in State Correctional down in Pittsburgh, but no, that part doesn't come until much later. For now, she is the young vessel of bliss, tripping fucked to the gills through the sweet, bright lights of corner stores, her nasal cavities still pink and glossy like the genitals of a young nun. Needless to say, the price of Kimmie's allegiance is not mere loyalty; the two have gone into business. Kimmie is the brains. Tillie is the money. Ames Iverson can be a very charming man.

*   *   *

Gordon is not given a cassock—or a monk name, for that matter. The Paterfamilias can't think of a more ego-destroying name than the one the boy walked in with, which the Pater imagines might be essential to the problem. Before the bell for silence, he tells the boy to sweep the temple. "All day?" Gordon asks. "It'll take you all day," the Pater explains. The temple has a roof but no walls, and because it's flanked by oak trees, there's really no end to sweeping it, even in summer when leaves aren't supposed to fall. Crickets seem to think of the temple as an auspicious place to die. "Our littlest pilgrims," Brother Van Loon calls them. Sweeping duty is always the first task assigned to a new monk; it diagnoses temper problems quite neatly.

As for temper problems, Gordon seems to have none. Even when Brother Itzhak walks through with a bag of flour slit in the corner so it spills out in dusty plumes, Gordon just starts again at the northeast corner and works his way through again. At lunch, Brother Sibelius sinks his thumb in Gordon's dish of lentils as he places it on the table and licks his warted thumb to punctuate the action, but Gordon smiles up past Brother Sibelius, in thanks to some grave divinity. The hazing is worse than the Pater anticipated, and responds elastically to Gordon's placid mien in the face of all kinds of minor abuse. Now, instead of flogging himself, he can instead give the whip to a stranger. Dwight B. causes the lone moment of distress in this arrangement when he tries, during the brief a.m. talk time, to draw out Gordon's troubles with his sympathetic ear. The Pater rectifies this distress by asking Gordon to carry buckets of water uphill from the stream using a yoke fashioned last-minute from two wooden coat hangers and electrical tape.

It goes against the Paterfamilias' general rules to devote so much attention to one of his charges, but he can't deny the kid is useful. The trouble will be, it seems, keeping the brothers from beating him with a sock full of nickels in retaliation for Gordon's bottomless reserve of patience. These men, after all, have been sent here because they formulated absolutely unnecessary responses to average civilians. That they know this about one another maintains a certain balance in the ranks. Chatter about who punch-fucked whom in which god-forgotten corner of Youngstown and so on is strictly verboten, yet goes on anyway and is tolerated to maintain this balance. The Pater steeples his fingers over a hot Dr Pepper in his study, charting the social forces pulling themselves into a noose of sorts. He calls up Ames Iverson's office in Erie with a freshly minted solution to the problem on his tongue, then visits Brother Dwight G. in his cell, where he has made a desk-sized facsimile of the town of Brigadoon as imagined in his childhood.

"Paterfamilias, to what do I owe the pleasure?" he asks.

"I need you to train Gordon."

"Gordon is good for nothing but shit. He ain't one of us." Dwight G. dabs glue on a cardboard hut with a toothpick to affix it.

"That's why I want you train him. Collections."

"Haw, haw, haw. That's pretty funny, Pater. No go."

"You think he couldn't do it?"

"Collections is easy. Like taking candy, pardon me for saying so, from a baby."

"No laundry gig for three months if you do it."

Dwight G. looks up from his handiwork with a smile that would suit a Santa Claus impersonator—same merry twinkle framed by little nose-pinching spectacles—and says, "Aw, gee, why didn't you say so?"

*   *   *

Gordon looks down at the bus ticket the Paterfamilias gave him the previous night, along with instructions to wake before the others and vacate. *Your skills have been noticed*, he was told, so he considered it a kind of promotion. Gordon thought he was executing his tasks capably and wonders why he is being dismissed to terrible Erie again, but the Pater instead gives him a slip of paper with an address written on it. This is where Gordon will stay. There, he will receive the address for the collection job. The phrasing sounds distinctly unmonkish.

The industrial low-slung buildings on either side of the bus route trouble Gordon with their dailiness. It had been a relief to narrow his field of vision to the tiles of the monastery or the slender ripples in the creek; the pointless labor let his shackled ideas wander away. The notion of anything having a point had seemed distant, but looking at the sad dregs of what people will just leave by the side of the road demands some kind of narrative. Dwight G. explained that the opposite of the collections job was empathizing, as if the reasons people did stuff mattered to you at all. "Act like that, you'll never be able to throw out a stuffed animal for your whole life," he had said. Gordon found this chilling as he retained his childhood stuffed animals in a garbage bag, which he had presently stashed in the crawlspace of his apartment. By now, he imagined his landlady had burned them, or maybe they would linger there a long time, unloved, cluttered up in the dark. No, no. He willed himself to see the vast steak he would consume after completing the job, the spry parsley next to it, the walleyed boobs of the waitress who would bring it to him. Imposition of one's will was the key according to Dwight G., which he drove home by giving Gordon a stack of index cards with various lies written on them. "We're not done here until you make me believe all of these," he had said.

Gordon did well with the ones that were a little more pedestrian. It wasn't hard to say "I like a ham at the holidays" or "The Dallas Cowboys are America's team," even if neither was particularly true; neither were they particularly false. But they progressed in difficulty until Gordon was intoning, "I am the unacknowledged legislator of hurt" and "I come from a long line of butchers" and "I'm a king and will do with you as I like" while Dwight G. landed insistent punches on his abdomen. Gordon keeps the cards on hand as if they will cue him in the process of making an actual collection, this first time from a very, very low-level and recent dealer who owes Ames Iverson $800.

He goes to an apartment over a tobacco shop in Erie's ersatz downtown zone, not actually very far from his old abode. Dropping his duffel in the closet, Gordon goes over the scanty cupboard and looks for generic implements to pass the time. Dominos in a vinyl carry case on the coffee table, a thoughtful touch in keeping a skin magazine called *Gun Butts* next to the toilet. It does nothing for Gordon, who convinces himself that he's more of a personality guy. He makes a cup of coffee and lights a cigarette, another element of Dwight G.'s teachings. According to Dwight G., cigarettes are one beginner avenue toward expressing your will such that it is thrown far before you like a tractor beam, and Dwight G. encouraged Gordon to heighten this effect by smoking in places where smoking is not allowed. Gordon opens the envelope propped next to the phone to receive his instructions. When he reads the name and address, he expels all his air in an astonished column. "Oh, mother of pearl," he says to no one.

*   *   *

Gordon drives the car left near the apartment to the assigned address. It's on the outskirts near the malls and the college. He tries to parallel the car in the cul-de-sac, decides it's pointless, and leaves it at a jaunty angle, unlocked. He walks up to Maryanne Phillips' house trying to figure out what to do with his hands. He lights a cigarette, hoping to exhale its ghost into a fierce cloak of armor for what he is about to do. One of the cars is gone, leaving a Rorschach of grease in the drive. A television's aquatic light burbles from a first-floor window.

He knocks instead of ringing the bell. Tillie Phillips looks through the glass panel at the top of the door, her hair in a loose, lolloping bun.

"Um," she says with the door cracked, "my mom's in the bath. So."

"I'm not here to talk to your mother."

"OK, um, so can I help you?"

"I'm here regarding a little business."

"Business?"

"Don't play the blushing dummy with me. Eight hundred." Gordon takes advantage of her stunned calculations—placing him within the purview of Ames Iverson, recalibrating her memory of the last time she saw Gordon, when he was desperate to eat his crab Rangoons in front of the TV in peace—to push past her into the white-carpeted foyer.

"You can't smoke in here."

"Really," he says, affecting a genuine personal interest in what she says. "OK, then." Gordon drops the lit cigarette onto the carpet. A little black pit hollows out under the cherry. He is beginning to enjoy this.

*   *   *

Deg is a young monk, brave and sweet. Also doomed. He has volunteered to embrace the wooden bell as it drifts from its moorings and moves tentatively toward a part of the horizon. Maryanne hopes that tonight she will find out how long he has the will to live. The rest of the islanders clutch doors, driftwood, whatever they can muster for survival. The garlands which had decorated the temple drift around them, a sad, sodden confetti of flowers. The islanders bear away their grief in song, in a lullaby.

Downstairs, Gordon seats himself on the white sofa and indicates for Tillie to sit next to him. He holds a pearl-handled butterfly knife, the Pater's very own, next to his cheek, tickles his sideburn with it.

"Now, Tillie, I don't know for the life of me why you would think Ames Iverson runs a charity operation." Tillie blanches. Her tan lines stand out from her skin like a ghost bikini.

"I don't have it." She says it so quietly.

"You do understand why I am here, though."

"Yes."

Gordon makes a row of incisions in the armrest. His face is etched by concentration. "You don't seem especially stupid to me."

"No." Tillie has regained a little control of her lower lip. "Let me get my mom. She can write you a check."

"You know what? That is a great idea. I'll go talk to her myself. You," he gestures with the knife, "stay right there."

The bathroom door stands open a crack from being repainted and repainted and warping in the humidity. Her head is on fire. Holy, holy, holy. Maryanne's breasts shine with oil. They are loose orbs hanging half in the water. Deg, the brave young monk, lets go of the bell as it drifts over a large breaker. He can't help it. The current drags him out to where the villagers cluster on their makeshift rafts, and the bell lets loose its million peals. It carries forth. It gets louder. Clearly, the villagers will die, and Maryanne is ashamed for what she has done to them. She weeps for every named thing.

Theft

Adam Gardner

Reid cupped his hands and blew into them while Nick held the wheel. They were driving through Iowa to the outskirts of Minneapolis. They'd heard their mother lived there. They wanted money.

"You even know what she looks like?" Nick asked.

"No."

"Dad says she's real pretty."

Nick touched his cheek with his glove. Reid watched him. Every so often their breath became visible in the moonlight. Outside the land was frozen and flat and silent. Reid imagined trying to dig into it and bruising his hands. There was a semi a few football fields ahead, but there could be nothing alive beyond it.

"Iowa should be burned. What's the point of it?" Nick said.

Reid nodded in a way that was serious. Running his hand across the dashboard, he spoke of numbness. He was boring always, he knew. Nick pushed the back of his head into the seat and closed his eyes. He seemed calm and almost to glow. He was the beautiful one, Reid thought. Besides the finger-shaped scar on his cheek, he had a face you could pray to.

Several of Nick's bangs were hanging across his eyelid. Reid brushed them with his forefinger, and Nick's eyes opened. The look was obvious—he was terrified.

"Hi, Mother. Nice to meet you. We're your sons," Reid said in a voice higher than his own.

"Hey, Mom. Give us some money."

They laughed and their breath was together for a moment. Reid pictured their mother's house as massive and clean. Nick closed his eyes again. Reid imagined him imagining her. He wanted Nick to cry and to ask him why he was crying.

"You know this is about us. Dad can find his own money," Reid said.

"I need clothes," Nick said, flicking the fringe lining a knee-hole in his jeans.

"A new truck is what I want. Maybe some CDs."

"I wouldn't want to touch her."

"No," Reid said, shaking his head. "No."

They'd been driving for three hours. Reid had promised not to drink and drive. He saw himself sneaking a sip at the next gas station. It didn't have to be necessary.

Soon enough it would be light out.

The truck shook as Reid got it up to ninety. Nick woke and smacked him on the shoulder. "Come on, don't," he said.

"Scared?"

Nick resumed his sleeping posture, and Reid eased off the pedal. He tickled the keys hanging from the ignition. Tired, he let the thought of getting his own place, moving out from his dad's, occupy him. If there were enough money, maybe he'd move to KC—even if he didn't lose his job at the lumberyard. People, when they cared, did things like that, he thought; they made leaps and became themselves. He saw himself staring out of an apartment window onto a busy street, waiting until someone looked up at him to return to the fridge and drink another and dream forcefully about how to take care of a day.

There were three actual deer ahead on the two-lane highway. Reid squinted his eyes and flashed his lights. Two hopped over the ditch and zigzagged across the blackened fields. One wouldn't move. Reid sped up and then braked and the tires screeched.

He pulled over and killed the engine. They'd clipped it.

"What the fuck?" Nick said.

"What?"

Blood leaked from Nick's forehead. In the windshield was a baseball-sized, spider-webbed crack. Reid wiped him with the sleeve of his coat. "My fault," he said.

He got out and inspected the truck. A headlight was smashed and the bumper dented. In the grill a tuft of gray fur shuddered. He patted the hood like it was a dog he'd yelled at too loudly and walked back to the deer. Behind him, the sun was just rising. A shiver ran through him. His brother opened his door. When Reid got to the deer, he could see its lungs moving beneath its ribs. He turned and yelled, "Not dead."

Nick walked quickly to the doe and knelt beside her. He put his head against the deer's ribs. The tiny stream of blood on his forehead turned, and Reid watched it advance just above his eyebrows. The deer's eyes brimmed; she was young still.

"Don't," Reid said. "Disease."

Nick kept his head on the deer. His face showed he could cry. Reid stood and un-tucked his flannel shirt and with his pocketknife cut a piece from the bottom of it. He placed it over the deer's eye.

"Why'd you do that?" Nick said.

"What do you mean?"

The piece blew off the deer and into the ditch; the deer blinked. Reid gripped through Nick's coat until he could feel his bicep tense and then he pulled him up and, with his arm around his shoulder, walked him to the truck and opened the passenger door. From his bag in the truck bed he grabbed a black t-shirt and tossed it at his brother and told him to wrap it tight around his head. He started the truck, turning its wheel counterclockwise until it stiffened.

"You're drunk?" Nick said.

"Jesus," Reid said.

Reid lined up on the opposing shoulder and put it in reverse until they were a good sixty yards away from where they'd pulled over. He pushed on the gas and eyed the RPMs and got ready for a thud and then it was there.

"There," he said.

They were back on the road, the sun now dark orange and almost full. They drove through a roadside town and saw a boy in an empty parking lot kicking a car's tire, his face scrunched against the invisible cold. From the window of the car a woman made a reasonable face. Reid squeezed Nick's thigh, just above his knee.

"If you need to cry," Reid said.

Nick looked at his brother as though he'd misheard him.

"I'm not drunk," Reid said.

They passed a few empty fast food restaurants and a church sign that told of gratitude for not being aborted. An image of his mother, in the cold air, peeling off his diaper came into Reid's head and repeated, as though a defect in a movie. She shook her head and smiled lightly, but he couldn't tell whether it was her actual face. His stomach tightened.

"You wonder why things are alive at all? Like why there isn't nothing?" Nick said.

"Because then we wouldn't be driving together to steal from mom," Reid said, punctuating it with a laugh, which he tried to make into a cough.

The deer had happened, and Reid couldn't breathe in the right way. He remembered speeding up, thinking the deer would move, realizing it wouldn't, and doing nothing. "Inevitable," he imagined saying if asked. But worse things now came to him—telephone poles, rock faces, guardrails—and he saw himself doing nothing, compelled. He coughed falsely again to have noise, but his breath shortened and as the cough took, he worried that it'd finally happened, that he'd become a secret from himself.

Talk. Please talk, Reid wanted to say. Instead he put his hand on the back of his brother's head, checking the t-shirt's knot. He let his palm run up and down the back of his scalp, through his thick, dark hair. His breath slowed. He felt lessened. "You probably got her hair," Reid said.

Nick shook his head back and forth like a dog when it wants to rip something from your grip.

Reid put both hands on the wheel and squinted at the black road and the tawny pastures and the round hay bales and abandoned barns giving into themselves. "You know, if you're gonna suck up to Dad and join the army, you need to get used to things dying."

"I might go to college."

"Money. You need money for that, Nick."

They crossed the Minnesota state line. Nick touched the scar on his cheek and looked at Reid. "You could go, too. Technical or whatever," Nick said.

For a second they made eye contact. Reid pulled off the highway and parked at a filling station. While the gas pumped he opened his bag and pulled out the whiskey. Clouds had bundled, but in the rifts between them sunlight penetrated. When Nick returned from the restroom, Reid tossed the plastic fifth to him and asked him if he'd ever had any. Nick shook his head. Reid grabbed the bottle from between his legs and twisted off the cap and handed it to him. "For your head," he said. "Just tilt it back."

Nick's eyelids clinched. "Don't watch me."

"It gets easier."

Nick took a decent swig. "It's burning," he said. "You?"

Reid took the bottle, held it close to his mouth, but spoke. "I have skills, you know."

"I know."

"Skills people go to school for."

Reid swallowed a little. He'd already taken a good pull, kneeling below the truck's bed gate. "That's all," he said. "I'm driving. You're not."

It was near noon when the Twin Cities first appeared in the distance. The sunlight was full, the sky open, and Reid felt there were reasons for things, that driving to his mother's house was what he should be doing, the next step in his twenty-seven-year-old life.

Dark conifers aligned the road, giving way occasionally to an iced pond or lake. Every ten or so miles, it seemed, there'd be a dead deer on the shoulder. Some had smeared the road with their insides; others looked as if they might stand and walk away at any moment. Nick had taken down a good third of the bottle and wouldn't stop patting the blood blotch on the t-shirt wrapped around his head.

"Maybe I don't want to do this," Nick said, his words almost chewed on.

Reid reached his arm around Nick's waist and pulled him close, to where their jeans were touching. His head drooped toward Reid's lap, and Reid lifted his chin with two fingers, staying it between the steering wheel and his chest.

"It's not stealing. We deserve it."

Nick raised his head and pushed himself back into his seat. "But jail," he said. "Jail would suck."

A woman passed them, staring at Reid the entire time. When he opened his mouth to yell, she was already a few cars ahead. His mother, he realized, could be anyone.

"You love her?"

"What?" Nick said. "No."

Reid untied the shirt from Nick's head. He pushed his knee against the wheel to hold it straight and folded the shirt and placed it behind his headrest. He let his fingers trace the outline of his brother's cheekbone. "You probably have her face, too. You have a woman's face."

Nick leaned away, resting his head on the passenger window. "Gross," he murmured.

Reid laughed. "You're scared, I know. But look at your face. That scar won't go away."

"Accident."

"Drunk, Dad said."

"Accident," Nick said louder.

"And then she left."

Reid put his hand underneath Nick's coat and pressed until he could feel the outline of his ribs.

"It's fun—you and me together. Soon you'll be leaving. And where will I be? I'll be working. I'll be with Dad."

Reid's two fingers tapped on Nick's ribs. They moved softly up his chest and pried into his armpit and wiggled. Nick huffed air out of his nose and inched away, squeezing his arm against his body so that only the tips of Reid's fingers remained in his armpit and trembled. Reid drew his hand back. They looked at each other. "Still ticklish?" Reid said.

Nick stared ahead, his face blank. Reid placed his hand over the hole in Nick's jeans and patted. "Used to have it bad," he said.

"What?"

"Ticklish."

Reid sucked his cheeks in and bit down on them. He wanted badly to say, "tickle, tickle, tickle" like their father used to when they became too quiet. He imagined saying it repeatedly, each time his voice a little higher, until his brother squirmed and laughed and said, "You're crazy." He removed his hand and rested it in his lap. "Hey, Mom," he let out. "You forgot us. Here we are."

Nick grabbed his hooded sweatshirt from below his seat and wadded it and set it against the passenger window and rested his head on it.

They exited the highway. Reid pulled out the crumpled directions from his coat pocket and smoothed them on his thigh. They still had at least an hour it looked like. They passed pawnshops, hair salons, laundromats, payday loan signs. He looked at his brother, who still stared straight ahead, his head resting on the window, and his jaw seeming almost to quiver, with what, Reid feared, was anger.

Reid shook his head and gave a long exhale. "You need to care about things," he said.

They came to a stoplight. A man who looked homeless crossed the street with two young girls, both in bubbly pink coats. All of them held hands. One of the young girls spit and glanced up at them and smiled. Reid smiled back, though too hugely, he felt, like a clown.

"So if she doesn't have anything?" Nick said.

"We'll take what she has."

Nick nodded his head slowly and then closed his eyes. Once it seemed he was asleep, Reid let his fingers walk down his brother's shin to the bottle on the floorboard. He wrenched it from underneath Nick's feet and looked around for cops. Seeing none, he took a long swig; when he saw himself in the rearview mirror he swallowed. He didn't like seeing his eyes, how wide open they were.

Their mother's house was not massive. It was a small, white home, no more than two bedrooms on a gravel road with a brown Buick in the driveway. Pieces of siding were missing from the front, and the roof over the concrete porch was caving in. The house was farther from Minneapolis than Reid had expected—the nearest neighbor was at least forty acres away. Twice he'd had to ask for directions. Several hula hoops lay in the front yard, which consisted of patchy dirt and leaves, and next to the garage sat a cracked toilet, ringed by yellow grass as tall as its bowl. Reid put his hand over his brow to read the wooden sign next to the front door. The words were carved in and painted red and said, We Don't Call 911. He imagined her nailing the sign up, looking around, pretending to laugh.

He tapped Nick's shoulder. "This is it. This is her house."

"Okay."

Reid placed a breath mint on his tongue and got out of the truck and walked to the front door and knocked. He listened to hear if the door would unlock before someone opened it. It didn't. She opened it just enough to fit her face out. She had Nick's pale blue eyes. Her face was tanned, its skin tight, and a few tiny wrinkles framed her thin lips. A memory of her humming, taking fruit from the fridge, flashed through him. She opened the door all the way. Under her beige shirt, her small breasts peaked, and he thought of the magazines his father would slide under his door. She said, "Yes?"

"My mother has cancer and I'm just going around the area, seeing if I can raise some money for her treatment. She's poor. We're very broke, I mean."

"Oh," she said. "Shit. Come in. It's cold."

Reid stepped onto a welcome rug with tiny blue birds and ivy on it and she shut the door behind him.

"The place," she said, and looked around, then at him. For an instant, her face seemed caught in fear, like no words could leave it. Then she laughed and said, "It's a mess, I'm sorry. I don't know what happened."

He scanned the room. There was a futon. There was a big-screen with a muted soccer game playing. On an end table next to the futon sat several diet soda cans, one with a cigarette butt resting over its opening. Above the fireplace hung a blue and turquoise tapestry, and on the mantle sat a gold-painted ceramic angel, a framed printing of the serenity prayer in its wings.

"Let me check my purse."

When she was out of the room, Reid turned the lock on the window behind the futon until it unsealed and went back to his place on the welcome mat.

She came out of the kitchen with a meek smile on her face. "This is what I can give."

She smoothed out three crinkled fives and then creased them before handing them to Reid. He held the bills between his thumb and middle finger. She stepped closer. His face warmed—her eyes seemed to move all over it. He looked down. She nodded her head slowly. Reid tried to smile and then somehow he was hugging her.

"Oh okay," she said.

He told her thank you. She rubbed circles into his back and said, "Sometimes they just want rest. Sometimes that's all."

Reid stepped back and turned and looked out the window to his brother in the truck. He could just make out his dark hair against the passenger window.

"You okay?" she said.

Reid nodded. His heart raced. "Yes," he said. "It's just hard."

"I know," she said.

"If you need work done I can do whatever—rake leaves, fix pipes, paint. For the money, I mean," Reid said, holding up the bills.

She smiled and stuck her small hands into her jean pockets and looked down. "I'm sure it seems I do, but I'm afraid I do just fine by myself."

"I'm sorry."

"No, I'm glad I could help."

Reid smiled and told her thank you and left.

It was after midnight when they returned. Reid clicked off the headlights when her house came into view and parked a few feet from her mailbox. Only the porch light was on. Reid rolled his window down. The wind blew strong, maybe enough to muffle their footsteps, and the air smelled of a far-away fire and his engine's slow burn of coolant. Above, beyond the barely lit moon, stars flooded the sky.

Reid turned off the engine and tried to find his breath. If he lost track of it, he felt sure he'd become trapped in himself. He told his shoulders to relax, and he eased them down; he looked at the house and envisioned her inside, her small face calm, dreaming. He knew she'd wake up to the theft and be unable to care. He could see her the next day, walking among the lost objects, peeking out the blinds at nothing, trying to hum but then stopping once her heart beat up to her neck. He could still make out where her hands had been on his back, the exact places—they almost burned. He took a sip from the bottle and then handed it to Nick. "You'll need some," he said. He wished they'd never come.

Nick shook his head.

"We're brothers. Come on."

Nick shook his head again and exhaled and took a small sip and sucked air through his teeth. "You're sure she didn't know?"

"It's been too long."

"But I don't know. Genes or whatever," Nick said and laughed a little.

"She's just a person," Reid said, trying to smile at his brother. He took the bottle back and rested it between his legs.

"Who made us."

"Exactly."

Reid undid his seatbelt. He found a good deep breath and scooted to the middle and placed his arm around his brother. He got his face close to Nick's. "If you're scared we can leave. We just won't ever do this again, you and me."

Nick knelt forward and traced the jagged perimeter of the crack in the windshield. He looked back at Reid. "I'm not scared," Nick said. "But you want me to be, I know."

Reid released his brother's shoulder. He held his mouth open as though to yawn, but when no breath came he said, "Hey."

"You do."

"How do you want me to be?"

Reid returned to the driver's seat. Nick lowered his head, forming a slack of skin under his chin, and closed his eyes halfway. In the dark of the cab he looked asleep. Reid studied him and waited for a movement or a word, but his brother remained still; only slow breath left him. He looked older, tired in an adult way, and Reid thought he could see the form Nick's face would take ten, twenty years from now. It felt almost like they shared nothing together and never had.

Reid touched the bruise on Nick's forehead, circled it, and Nick inched away. "I'd recognize you," Reid said.

"What?"

"If you left is all I mean."

"I'm not."

"But college or whatever."

"Jesus."

Reid took another drink, but had to swallow quickly because his breath let out. He felt as though he were panting. He looked at his brother to see if he noticed, and in the way he looked back Reid could tell that Nick was afraid of him, afraid of what he might do. Reid reached out to touch his brother's shoulder, to simply pat it and tell him it was okay, but Nick squished himself to the door and then opened it and the cab light came on. "I'm ready," he said.

Reid nodded and kept nodding until he heard himself say, "We don't have to."

Nick got out of the truck and lightly shut his door and walked across the yard. Reid watched him, waiting to see him stumble and fall or turn around. When Nick got within a few feet of the house, Reid got out and hurried to his brother.

They went in through the front window. Nick had the kitchen, Reid stuck to the living room. She had little, but they gathered what they could quietly get through the window—a tapestry, some CDs, silverware, olive oil, *People* magazines, a ceramic angel, beaded necklaces, speakers, and a tiny turquoise bear. Reid took the last load to the truck and sat now in the driver's seat, watching the window, expecting at any moment to see the dark shape of his brother emerge and walk toward him.

He took a sip of whiskey, eyeing the remainder as he swallowed. He was careful to leave a good ounce. His breathing felt right, but he knew it could leave him at any moment—where was his brother? He told himself that if she found him the lights would be on. There would be noise, voices, unquiet emotions. He turned away from the house for a bit, hoping, but when he turned back his brother was still not approaching. "Passed out, is all," he made himself say aloud. Her holding Nick, her eyes warm and teary, her fingers in his hair, all of that entered him. But at least one light would be on, he told himself. He thought of carrying his brother out, a drunk, sleepy smile on Nick's face. He'd let him sleep. He began to count up to a minute, then he stopped and got out and went to the window and gathered himself in.

Except for a red dot on the bottom of the TV the living room was dark. Reid whispered his brother's name but then placed his hand over his mouth. He turned on his flashlight and ran the light over the edges of the room. From her bedroom down the hall a television still played, its blue light flashing through the space at the bottom of the door, its excited voice barely audible. He stepped into the kitchen. The cupboards and drawers were all still open. Dishes were stacked in the sink and smelled faintly of sour milk. He whispered Nick's name again and then walked down the hall and checked the bathroom, slowly gliding the shower curtain back. He wanted to scream his brother's name. He went across the hall to his mother's bedroom and opened the door. It creaked barely. He got down on his hands and knees and scooted toward the bed. When he came to the foot of the bed, he got up on his knees.

The TV light fluttered over both of them. She was on the left side of the bed, facing the wall. His brother was next to her, facing her back, his nose nearly in her hair. He placed his hand on Nick's leg and squeezed it, but Nick didn't move. He moved on his knees to Nick's side of the bed. He guided his hand down Nick's back, over his coat, until he came to a loophole in his jeans. He hooked his index finger through the loophole and stood and pulled. Nick turned his head up and shook it.

Reid removed his finger and mouthed, "Come on," but Nick turned away and placed his head back on the pillow.

"Please," Reid said.

Their mother moved. "Hello," she said softly, then coughed. "Hello?"

Reid stepped quickly out of the bedroom without looking back. He crawled out the window and went to his truck and started it, resting his foot on the gas, eying the house. After a few minutes he rolled the window down and turned off the engine. He stuck his head out. There was no noise except for the wind and the house was completely dark.

Reid woke in the morning to his heart knocking. The sun was almost full behind her house and the clouds moved toward him. He put a breath mint in and squeezed his eyes together. He tried to look at himself in the rearview mirror; his pupils were full. He turned and looked in the bed of the truck, Nick wasn't there. He got out and went to the window but it was now locked shut and the blinds were down. He went back to the truck and in two trips carried her stuff to the front porch and stacked it neatly by the front door. He stood by the door; his breath left him like smoke. There was a breath below his breath that he needed and he kept his mouth open, waiting for it. He raised his arm to knock on the door but then lowered it. He whispered his brother's name and then said it aloud several times. He said it again. He pressed his ear against the door and heard a creak, a movement. He told himself he'd leave when he heard his brother's voice.

Berserker

Megan Clark

No one knew who or what this boy was. If he could talk, then he'd call himself a bat, a flightless one. In a futile gesture, he flapped his arms as if they were wings, but never ascended any higher than his sad jumps to catch air. Instead of flying, he scuttled about in the dark, crouching, keeping his body close to the walls and floors, ensuring that he didn't appear vulnerable and unprotected. He lacked a cloud of bats to call his own and one that might include him in their nocturnal swooping across the skies.

A group of men found him in a cave; they were from town, investigating a dark opening cut into the hillside and hoping to find valuable artifacts left behind. Instead they found the boy, sleeping away the day deep inside the cave where no ray of sunlight would reach him, and at first the group believed him to just be another dirty rock until he rolled over and jerked away, scared of their heavy boots and bright flashlights. He screeched, high-pitched wailings that bounced off the cave's close quarters, stirring a few of his leathery-winged brethren to flap confusedly over the group, causing one man to pull a revolver from its holder and wave it around futilely. The man never fired off a shot, but the boy continued his own bat-like lamentations until the man silenced him with a swift pistol whip to the back of the head.

He lay silent and the men carried him out of the cave, not excited by their find. They very well couldn't sell him as they had hoped to do if they found various relics. This strange boy had thin, sallow skin, but the soles of his hands and feet were nearly black from grime. He was naked except for the wild tangle of rusty hair that bloomed on his scalp; they decided he couldn't be any older than eleven or twelve. They loaded him in the back of their truck and decided that the Baptist church should take him since they ran a food pantry and knew about helping people in need.

The Baptist preacher, joined by the Methodist pastor, eagerly accepted responsibility for the boy, because it was clearly their duty to introduce him to civilization and to the light of Jesus Christ, since they doubted that God had come to the boy in the darkness of that cave and if anyone needed saving from Satan, it was a scrawny, dirty boy who had probably never seen a church. They scrubbed him clean with Ivory soap, the water turning gray before he gleamed whiter than a lady's pearl necklace. He fought them the whole time, so the pastors conspired to cut his hair, while he slept, into a jagged mop. They managed to shove a men's shirt over his head, but he refused to wear pants, ripping them and popping the buttons clean off. Thankfully, the cotton shirt was too long on him and fell nearly to his knees. Despite the pastors' best efforts, the boy remained unreceptive to their talking and the shiny leather Bible that they read to him from. The boy did not respond to his newly given name, Adam, which meant to suggest the boy's primitive genesis. He preferred crouching in the basement among the musty cardboard boxes filled with Christmas tinsel and Communion linen. He'd only ascend the stairs to the sanctuary when the sun had fully set and the dirt-streaked windows grew full dark. The Baptist preacher kept him locked in the parsonage at night for fear he'd escape back into the wild.

Churchwomen tittered over him, continually blessing his heart, while he hunkered behind pews, peering over the seats with his wide, milky eyes, which were like two full moons with inviolable craters for pupils. The women gladly volunteered to compare the boy's picture to those of missing children from the tri-county area. None of them matched him, though one seemed close, same lean face and penetrating stare, but the family had moved after their loss and no one knew where they had resettled. Gagging on every casserole pressed into his mouth, the boy sucked down only cold water at first, then cans and cans of tuna fish. Later, when they found him eating raw, bloody hamburger meat meant for the upcoming chili supper and saw the squiggles of pink beef littering the white lace tablecloth, the pastors could take no more. He would not speak, he would not listen, he would not be baptized (they'd already tried with disastrous results, since the Baptist had insisted on immersion)—now this. He had learned how to use indoor plumbing, how to light the gas stove when the sanctuary grew cold, how to open his own cans of tuna. But they grew tired of padlocking the icebox, of shooing him out of the kitchen, of his strange crouching and arm flapping, of his daily climbing of the sanctuary rafters, which scared the congregation. This boy was clearly a lost cause and they needed to get back to those who were receptive to their message of cleanliness and godliness.

Too scared to contact the government (what horror would he wreak on an orphanage?) or burden their flock, they collectively decided he couldn't go back to his cave, that was uncivilized, and he needed to be watched over. There was only one place they could take him; he could go live with the Lady. The pastors even tacitly agreed that he somewhat resembled her. So, wrapped in a blanket, the boy sat in the back of the coroner's hearse, the only public service vehicle with blacked-out windows, and bumped along a back road until the double doors swung open. The Methodist pastor took his left arm while the Baptist took his right. Then they walked him to the front door of a sprawling pillared house, a mansion if one were inclined, on a desolate estate that hadn't seen the attention of a gardener in ages. It was nearly dark, but the boy still trembled at the last red-gold light lingering in the western sky. He kept silent as if sensing that this was a place he didn't have the privilege of squeaking. The two men dropped the boy on the wide porch supported by crumbling columns, returned to the hearse and drove away, bouncing in the potholes that marred the deserted road. They were glad to be rid of him.

Inside lived the Lady, the very last of her family, and the brass plaque next to the door stated VOLBLOED - 1845. The boy smelled the scent of tangy copper that hung about the doorway and the weathered white steps, though they were not red with blood. He now knew about doors, and turning the knob, found the entryway unlocked. Sniffing along the floorboards, he followed the smell of blood, the smell of food through the foyer, down a series of hallways, into a wide kitchen with dusty pans hanging from the ceiling. To the left, the kitchen had a door to the backyard where the sun's corona was slowly being consumed by a sea of trees. The boy, unsure of what lay outside, opened the door to his right, which lead to a subterranean darkness. Feeling the sweep of cool air on his skin, he instinctually followed the darkness and the cold and the smell of blood into the cellar that had served the Volbloeds for over a century. The black space enveloped him, lulling him into a state of calm that had never happened in the pristine, clean-smelling church. Curled beneath a table, he succumbed to sleep despite the oncoming night. The reverends had nearly switched his circadian rhythm to what they deemed normal. With his temple pressed to the dirt floor and his breathing now even, the boy did not acknowledge the sound of a bolt sliding into place and the click of lock, the same noise he heard while at the parsonage.

At first, he wasn't alarmed when he couldn't leave the cellar; it was dark and cool and nice. But he also knew how doors were supposed to work and this one wasn't working properly. So he tried again. And again. And again. Finally, he began keening at the barred entrance until the door opened. A blindingly bright figure backtracked as he exited the cellar. The Lady, in an all white gown complete with bustle and corset, stood in front of him and her hair rose above her head in a high coiffeur. She reached into a sack and carefully removed a calf's leg, careful to pick it up so that the fresh meat didn't dribble blood onto her outfit. Wordlessly, she held it out to him. He cowered, and then too hungry to hold out, he grabbed it and began tearing at the flesh. While he was chewing a large piece, she said, "I thought that's what you'd like." He didn't respond, just kept eating. "Let me ask you, did those two charlatans talk about the fruits of the spirit?" He gnawed at the exposed metacarpus and gazed at her as she continued talking. "You look clean, but I can smell where you've been. I saw the look in your eyes," she pointed to her own eyes then to the cellar, "as you tracked that scent and hoped to find more at the bottom of that hole." She crumbled the stained paper sack. "They think their god only creates good, but here you are. Here I am." She left the boy to his meal and walked out of the kitchen and into the encroaching blackness outside.

After that night, she didn't lock him in the cellar again. She didn't halt him from following her up the staircase and she didn't shut any doors behind her. She didn't stay in the house long after the moon appeared and she left him alone for long stretches of time. Human company was still new to him, and he did not miss such interaction. He had only felt loneliness when he was away from the bats, when the bats left his cave and he could not follow them into the sky. While living in the cave, he had seen larger mammals: deer, coyotes, and bobcats, but shied away from them, scared. He once tried to approach a doe, a quivering hand outstretched to touch it, but it had bounded away. The bats were near to him, close, yet never threatening; they never bit him as a mangy coyote had once. He often thought of returning to his cave, the safe, dark place with the rush of wings and chirping of bats. Thrice, he ran away to find his home cave again. He tore off his shirt before dashing into the woods, his bare body burning in the cold air. No matter how much he searched, he always became turned around in the dark woods and barely found his way back to the house. The stars burned bright in the sky each escape, yet he couldn't manage to discover the jagged opening in the hillside. The third time he sat in a tree on the edge of the mansion's back lawn, feeling the cold bite more sharply and the bark scratch his back. All the leaves were gone and only the night stretched above him. A single candle burned in an attic window; it stayed lit until the sky lightened and the boy returned to blow it out.

Before they took the precaution of locking him in the church, the preachers knew when he'd fled to seek the darkness of his cave and dragged the boy back. The Lady never tracked him down, never forced him back to the cellar. She looked knowingly whenever she returned home to find him inside, staring out one of the attic's many windows. Soon, the attic became his second haunt, after the cellar. The beams crisscrossing the rafters were sturdy enough for him to hang from them. He relished the feeling of blood rushing to his head and would linger there long after he knew the Lady had reentered the house. He chirped at any bat that dove by the windows and kept the glass pane open so he could stretch out his hand to those that flew close.

Toward the rear of the house was a large ballroom with a set of chairs and a black four-poster bed with white sheets, dragged to face the room's largest fireplace by the Lady from her previous bedroom in the east wing. The rest of the long ballroom remained empty of furniture, nothing sat in front of the opposite fireplace. Noises echoed loudly off the scuffed hardwood floors that had once been polished by dancing feet. Mounted animal heads lined the ballroom's walls; a vast array of deer, elk, and moose grinned down from beneath their antlers. All were dust-covered except for one. High above the largest fireplace hung a shining wolf pelt, glossy black peppered with flecks of gray. The head was attached and laid flat against the wall, deflated, though its ears still stood upright. When she awoke, the Lady took the wolfskin down, brushed the fur until it gleamed, and most often hung it back on the wall. Sometimes, the boy heard her singing and peered into the room. There the Lady lounged, holding the wolfskin in her lap, and sang brightly to it, while she brushed it. The boy would silently slide to the floor and mimic her motions as he ran his fingers through his hair like a comb.

The Lady looked like someone had pulled very fine, pale silk over a razor skeleton. She, like all those before her, had an aristocratic pointed nose, pointed elbows, and pointed chin, but she'd survived the longest. Her true name had fallen away and died with disuse, so she went by the Lady, a name of respect and fear. She moved with an impeccable posture, her spine a steel rod. Her movements through the house were graceful whether she was on two feet or all fours (but it would be weeks before the boy saw her stalking along the ground and howling in her wolfskin). When he first arrived, she appeared immaculate, gliding about the front hallway in crushed velvet gowns one day and full-skirted swing dresses the next. She appeared in corsets, in fringe, with shoulder pads, with torpedo brassieres. She rouged her pale cheeks and thin lips while her eyes were lined thickly with black. All the clothes smelled like mothballs, so the boy kept a wide berth from her. He only came closer when she appeared at the door with a fresh kill—a doe or a jackrabbit—and a double-barrel shotgun slung over her shoulders, carefully applied lipstick staining her mouth while her riding pants remained spotless. She smoked her cigarettes in a fine ebony and gold holder, perching the slim instrument between her middle and pointer finger. She would direct him with its burning tip to store the rest of the fresh kill in the cellar, which grew cooler and cooler as winter approached.

The people in this county have a particular nursery rhyme that they teach their children. "The Lady is out tonight," they croon down to their toddlers. "Lock your doors and keep them tight. Or else she'll snatch you up before morning light." The children then huddle under their blankets as their parents laugh softly and turn out the bedroom light. But afterward, when the children have fallen asleep, the mothers and fathers check their front and back doors to make sure they are locked as well, because they've heard that rhyme their whole life and realize how true it is. Dogs go missing, cattle, sometimes horses, and rarely, very rarely, a little boy or girl, most often in the deep of winter.

Early one morning, not long after having been abandoned, the boy heard a knock on the front door. The Lady descended the stairs and then peered through a yellowed lace curtain. The knock came again, causing the boy to jump. She came into the kitchen, shushed him, and shoved him out of sight. "Stay low," she whispered and pushed down on his shoulders until he crouched. At the kitchen tap, she ran water over her face, along her teeth, and smoothed back her hair. She gave him a final stern look before opening the door. The cold morning air rushed in, ruffling her nightgown. The boy, squatting behind the kitchen island, peered around the corner and held up a hand to block some of the bright light spilling into the house.

"What can I help you with, deputy?" the Lady asked and smiled with her teeth fully bared.

The deputy was young, a fresh recruit, with a single scuff on his shiny black shoes. He clicked his pen and prepared to take notes. "We're out canvassing the area for a young girl," he said. "Name's Lila Melton, gone missing since last night. About this high," he motioned at his waist, "with red hair, blue eyes, wearing a pink coat and boots. Have you seen her or have any information on her whereabouts?"

"Can't say that I have. I'm sorry." The deputy peered around the Lady's arm that propped the door open and she maneuvered to block his view.

"We're sweeping the woods right now. Their land is just adjacent to yours. Are you sure you haven't seen anything? We think yours would be the first house she'd come upon if she ran this way."

"Like I said, I haven't noticed anything out of the ordinary, but

"Ma'am, do you mind if I come in and look around?"

"Yes, I very much mind if you do that, though I'm not intractable. Keep sweeping my woods, but I don't think you'll find the girl alive. It's cold and many nasty things lurk at night. Take your hand off my property."

The deputy paused then slowly lowered his arm and stepped back. His lips parted slightly and his eyes looked confused. "I'm sorry, ma'am," he said.

"Good, you should be. Disturbing me, accusing me." She smiled. "Deputy Harmon, what I want you to remember is that I haven't anything to do with this girl or with you. I want you to leave and remind your superiors that I'm to be left alone." The deputy began shaking. "Are you scared?" she asked. He nodded. "Good, remind them that they should be too." Cheerfully, she dismissed him. "Find that girl's body. It won't be anywhere near here."

Deputy Harmon turned away and pulled his coat tighter around his shoulders, as his forefathers had done and their fathers before them. She watched from the door as the cop car reversed out of the weeds and sped out of sight. Shutting the door, the Lady knew the sheriff would reaffirm that she should be left alone to live as she pleased. There would be no wolf tracks leading them to the girl or any that led directly to the Lady's house.

She found the boy still in the kitchen and he rose as she approached him. Holding his chin in her fingertips, she inspected his features then let him go.

"You wouldn't have wanted to go back with them," she said. "Those people, not even able to take care of their own. Such a shame."

After the visit, the Lady stayed in several nights, a strange anomaly, and one night, she sat him at what had once been a magnificent dining table. The scent of her clothing and her cigarette smoke nauseated him, but her eyes dared him to move. "I don't know what happened to make you so afraid of trousers, but you are being absurd. If your tail freezes to that seat, I won't help free you. You'll just have to wait and thaw," she said and took the chair opposite him.

She lit a single taper in the bone-white candlestick, bright enough to see by, but not so much that they squinted in the glare. The Lady didn't need a candle to see, but sometimes human habits were hard to break and a light did offer a kind of comfort. The table was glossy under years of dust. Long scratches and bite marks marred it. The boy sniffed at them and found them to be old and odorless. She watched him over the candle flame. The temperature in the house dropped steadily, and their breath mingled with the smoke and rose toward the high ceilings.

She moved a tray with tea service in between them; steam now mixed with their breath and the smoke as she poured them two cups. The teapot had been silver, but was now patina; roses blossomed on the china with gilt running along the edges. She traced a finger along the handle. "This was my sister's favorite, so don't break it. She was my only sister and I don't have much to remember her by. You'll want sugar in yours."

She held up a single sugar cube then dropped it into his cup. The boy sniffed at the offering and held his hand over the heat radiating from it. Delicately, the Lady mimed taking a drink. "Don't gulp it down like you do a squirrel." He followed suit, scalding his tongue on the heat and the bitterness. "And don't give me that look. You can tell it's hot, I haven't tricked you. Cool it off." She mimed blowing on her tea and added another sugar cube to his cup. He did the same and soon motioned for another cup with three sugars, prompting her to keep adding the cubes until he was satisfied. "See it's not so bad." She continued her pantomime of drinking, though her cup always stayed full and she allowed him to finish most of the tea on his own. The smallest of smiles turned her lips.

This pretext of civility fell away at the end of that month. She started wearing high-waisted black slacks and a tucked-in red shirt that had been another color before; she looked more comfortable, more natural in them. The boy, at ease with such earthy smells, sniffed it and lapped at the sleeves until she jerked away and clobbered him across the cheek. Maybe she had lived with decorum when her sister had been alive, when she had more refined company to share her home with, when they pretended to hold balls and dressed in extravagant gowns and simpered over glasses of stale champagne, when they'd been accepted into the social circles of the town and hosted people in their home. What did she have now? A homeless child that could only squeak instead of speak, that gazed up at her from his crouched position with eyes that looked like telescopes zooming in on her once celestial face.

But when the quarter moon rose, that's when the boy saw her naked. At first, having never been barred from any room, he scratched at the locked door to her bedchambers. He pressed his eye to the keyhole and watched as the Lady stripped to her thin, naked flesh. Looking at her still, he touched his now seemingly strange flattened chest and pressed against his groin to be sure he remained intact. Her shoulder blades stood out sharply as she reached over to the bed where the wolf pelt lay. She threw it over her bare shoulders and hunched down onto the floor. The pelt stretched and stretched until it consumed her, until she sat up on four paws and twitched her ears and then howled at having become a wolf.

After the boy saw her transform, he hid in the attic and waited for her return. Broken mirrors and looming furniture seemed to crowd him suddenly. He stumbled over a rusted shield and a broken quiver of arrows. Avoiding the windows, he began digging about in the deep trunks. Inside, he found carefully packed fur-trimmed capes, woolen dresses, and eventually a ratty gray uniform, complete with jacket, vest and trousers. The buttons and tassels were tarnished, but the fabric was still intact and seemed warm. A strange rusty stain emitted from where the heart would lay under the coat. The Lady scowled whenever she saw his naked legs and he shied away from her whenever she did so. Pants restricted his motion; it was harder to jump and hang upside down wearing them, but having lived in houses, he'd grown soft and the cold pained him more than it used to. So now, he tucked his long dress shirt into the trousers, pulled on the coat and buttoned it. The pants and coat sleeves were too long so he rolled them up. He admired himself in the fragments of a gilded mirror. His face nearly looked as sharp and bloodless as hers; he touched the contours, noting the colors, and thought of the Lady's face. If a person compared the two, they might say that she had borne him and left him in that cave, many years ago, and maybe that was why the pastors had left him on her doorstep.

Peering down the staircase through the railing, he watched as she stumbled back onto the second-floor landing, the wolf pelt loose around her shoulders with blood and dirt caking her hands and mouth, like dark, smeared lipstick. The stink of deer hung about her. Her glazed, red eyes barely registered him and his outfit.

The next time, two weeks later, she did not close her door, not caring if the boy saw the pelt consume her as her body rearranged into an animal. She did not glance at him as she padded out of the house and into the night.

Finally, after the third time, he followed her out. He was used to the small copse that lay beyond the wild back lawn and he trailed her doggish scent there. She had stopped bringing him any kills and snarled at him as best she could with her human mouth if he tried to take a turkey or a raccoon from her, so he loped out into the forest, never daring to go as far as she did, and was able to keep himself satisfied on the squirrels and possums. He was very adept at climbing trees and sitting still; squirrels and other small mammals, never smelling human on his flesh, ran right over his hands and made quick meals of themselves. The trousers did get in the way, but he enjoyed staying warm more. When she had first realized what he'd been wearing, she had attempted to take it off him. "You can't have this. You can't wear this. My father didn't serve for some little boy to parade around in his uniform." She had pointed back up the stairs to indicate that he should find something more suitable to wear. She had touched the small round hole in the breast of the coat and the few fine gray fibers that emitted from amidst a dark bloodstain; she looked at his face and as she did so, relented and said, "Fine, keep it, but don't disgrace it." He was glad of the clothes now as he followed her scent deeper and deeper into the woods.

The boy did not catch up to her; her four limbs far outpaced his two. Instead, she caught him unawares as he crouched next to a stream, a thick frost on the ground and him without shoes on. The boy had already feasted on a rabbit and had then been startled by his own reflection in the water. He had leaned over to peer closer, to see how wild his hair had become, how purple the crescents under his eyes. Without warning, she nipped his heels, the right, the left, back to the right, over and over. Nearly collapsing into the freezing water, the boy did a wild dance as he backed away from her. He felt her pointed teeth graze across his skin and cried out when one pierced his ankle in her haste. She continued biting, biting, biting at him until the old mansion loomed just beyond the trees. Finally, she stopped and stood, her breath rolling out in thick pants as her tongue lolled to the side. The boy made as if to touch the furry crown of her head, as if to bury his fingers in between her ears. For such intentions, she snapped at him, bloodying his pale hand as her long canines tore across his knuckles. Instead of his fingers, trails of blood descended into her black fur, indistinguishable in the darkness. After she awoke from her oblivion-like sleep, these trails were dried on her forehead and she scrubbed them off before the boy saw them. Because, of course, he came back.

The Lady resumed serving the boy tea, and she had also brought a plain wooden box and dumped its contents onto the table. Misshapen pieces of wood thumped and scattered between them. She quickly flipped them over, revealing shades of faded blue, green and brown. With ease, she fit together two pieces and then a third and then a fourth. He gazed at her ability to do so and watched as she assembled all the various pieces into a whole, a slightly rounded rectangle that displayed the continents and the oceans. Sea monsters roamed in the blue areas; their eyes bulged and their horns reared above the inky waves. A long, thin ship with billowing sails moved from one landmass to another.

"My family came a long, long way." With her finger, the Lady traced from a small island near the top, through the sea, sailing until it hit the label "New World."

"I was fine, but my sister hated being on the boat. She would have liked you. Though not in a good way." She studied the boy. "Maybe it's best she died. She liked the taste of little boys and girls, always got us in trouble when we least needed it. We hated what she did, where was the honor in killing children? But we loved her and so we didn't stop her." Lines appeared around her eyes as she scrutinized him. "Do you know death? My sister has been dead for years, but it feels fresh, like every dawn I will find her body again and again and again. Men and their guns. There aren't any wars now, but they are still thirsty to kill something."

She began snapping the puzzle pieces apart and scooping them back up into the box before he could lay a finger on them. "That hunter left her there to die after he shot her, left her there soaked in her own blood, but took the pelt off her back. He said that he hadn't seen her, that he'd been mistaken. He was scared when he realized what he'd done, but he said that she was crazy for slinking around the woods at that hour. She was an animal, he told me, she was a wolf. He swore it. All I remembered was howling and howling. I dragged her body home that morning, then I showed him an animal. I showed him death."

With force, she slammed the box closed and did not look at him. "Put this in the attic." She pointed up for emphasis, though the boy showed recognition of his hiding place. He tucked it away where only he could find it and when she left him alone, without tea or company, he returned to the box, opened it and stared at the pieces, and equated them with the Lady's downturned mouth and fiery eyes. He was too scared to take them out, in case he put them together but in entirely the wrong order.

The boy, with his little experience with gas stoves and with the Lady's prodding, learned to build and feed a fire, much like any other boy who was not raised in a cave. The Lady's bedchamber glowed, because he stoked the embers when she was out late. Now, its heat engulfed her as she stood in front of it, peering above the fine marble mantle. Growing hotter and hotter, she ripped the skin from the wall, but instead of petting it as expected, she tore at its paws, its limbs, its ears, its eye sockets. She raged at it. She bit at it with her human teeth and tried to rend it with her useless human fingernails. Panting, she stopped and looked up at the blazing fire. The flames lit her eyes and reflected as a lamp behind frosted glass, bright and cold. Then she seized the wolfskin, crumpling it into an inelegant ball, and dangled it just beyond the flames' reach. Her arm shook, the pelt quivered in her grasp, shining in the red light. She reared back once, twice, a third time, muttering *kasta* as if to imbue herself with the willpower to throw the pelt into the fire once and for all, but she could not bring herself to do so.

Having heard her grunting and moaning, the boy descended from the attic, half expecting her to be a wolf though it wasn't the right night for her change, but he only saw her human form crouched by the fireplace. She wept tearlessly; her tears had dried up years ago. She was dressed in a wide, shapeless shift, yellowed with age. Her face was plain and her hair undone around her shoulders. She saw him hovering, only half his face awash in firelight as he stared at her, and her face twisted into rage, her angles hardening. But this too changed, a softening of the jaw, an unclenching of the teeth, and she thrust the pelt at him, saying, "*Taka skinn. Taka.*" He backed away from her.

She continued muttering in the strange guttural language, one harsher and more lyrical than the English spoken in the church, where the women spoke in soft tones. She bit the consonants and rolled through her speech like a long ship crashing along choppy waves. Most often she said, "*Drepa mig, drottinn. Drepa mig.*" She held her hands upwards to the high, dark ceilings and kept pleading in the strange tongue, the wolf pelt held aloft as if in offering. Eventually, her eyes regained their usual sharp focus and she shuddered, pulling the skin close to her, retracting swiftly from the fire and crashing into her bed. "*Fararleyfi,*" she said and then remembering whom she spoke to, she corrected herself. "Leave." The boy whimpered by the door, clearly unsure about leaving her alone, worried that she might fall back into that feverish trance, maybe fling herself into the fire instead of the pelt. He hesitated. "Have you gone deaf? Are those huge receptors for ears not working? *Hvat?* Answer me." She yelled the last part, nearly bringing an angry blush to her cheeks. Turning pallid again, she waved him out the door. "Leave." He obeyed her this time, fleeing into the cellar to seek the comfort of the familiar smells and darkness, but he could not sleep; he passed out from exhaustion as the sun hit the highest point in the sky.

It was several days before she spoke to him again or even acknowledged his presence. In the chilly interim, the house felt darker and this would not have troubled the boy except now he had grown used to candlelight and fireplaces and her presence. He delayed going inside; the Lady would be out, roaming the woods, in whichever form and though the house was bigger than his cave, it sometimes felt smaller. So when the boy's stomach was full, instead of going inside, he flapped about in the backyard, still trying to gain air beneath his bony arms. He contemplated trying from a higher distance, but he held back. In the cave, he had contented himself with being near his brethren; now he looked enviously from windows or tree branches, at that seemingly infinite space of air in which he could jump and fly. The boy remained satisfied with jumping about, his breath leaving a misty trail behind him.

Inside, he lit a single candle, a red one he found lodged in a sconce. Sitting out for him were several sugar cubes and a single cup of tea, like a ceramic white flag. She had not bound his hand; he had done that, clumsily, with strips torn from his shirt.

Immediately after tying his bandages, the boy had scooped up the wooden box with the puzzle and hidden it among his nest of clothes and blankets in the attic. Two pieces sat atop the rest; he had snapped them together properly, their irregular joints forming to spell the word "New" across a green background.

This delicate peaceful period was broken when the boy heard a crack, crack, like the sound of a tree limb snapping after an ice storm. The Lady had stayed out later than she normally did, even for a night with a half-moon, but the boy had not followed her, instead looking down at the pink scars crisscrossing his white knuckles. He knew better. As he considered going down to the cellar to sleep (the attic was drafty), a howl resonated from deep in the woods; it sounded scared. The boy stumbled down the stairs and out the back door, the one he spotted his first night when he was still too scared to escape. His hat nearly flew off his head with the force of his running; it was a faded gray kepi cap with two tarnished swords crossed above the flat bill. He'd rescued it from the cavernous attic and liked that it matched his coat. She was running toward him, her shaggy paws pounding the ground. A darker shape followed close behind. It was the Baptist preacher with a rifle, harrying her, refusing to give up chase, despite how much she outpaced him. The boy slowed down at the sight of the man—his dark hair obscured by an orange cap, his breath ragged from trying to keep up with her, his hands red from the cold. Those were the same hands that had held the boy underwater until he struggled for breath then brought him back to air with both men smiling.

Not knowing what else to do, the boy yelled at the preacher. He trilled and whooped and hollered. Stutterings of the word 'no' interspersed his screaming that turned his neck a deep red. The preacher skidded to a halt in the morning frost; he looked shorter dressed in drab brown than when he was dressed in his black suit and tie. He made as if to raise his rifle and take another shot, but a slow realization dawned across his face. He stopped watching the wolf and looked at the boy, the one he had taken in and then abandoned, but he struggled to recognize him and could only see the image of a long-dead Confederate soldier, obviously too young to enlist, too poor for shoes, who died from a shot to his chest, who was paler than death itself. The boy continued yelling and chirping at the preacher, waving his fists in his direction, no understanding of the black metal that was cradled in his hands. Ignoring all rules of hunting safety, the preacher ran away, swinging his rifle to and fro; his jostling caused him to squeeze the trigger and discharge the round into the bare branches. A flock of birds ascended and flew toward the oncoming white-rimmed horizon.

A bullet had grazed the Lady's arm, but the wound was not deep and had already clotted. The boy helped her into the house. She leaned on his shoulder and their faces, bobbing next to each other as they stumbled, looked like two halves of the same wan moon. He led her down into the cellar, there were too many stairs to her bedroom, and placed her in the corner farthest from the windows, where he liked to lay, where the light would not reach her. The boy pulled the wolf pelt around his shoulders and smelled the mixture of human and beast in the fur, a smell of something in between, of something kindred.

The Erratic

Christina Milletti

Dilly was ten, or maybe eight, or possibly twelve years old the day she disappeared, for the last time, from her engineered neighborhood on Willow Park Lane. She no longer remembered when the final vanishing happened. Long ago, maybe yesterday, she sat alone in the backyard of her home where a large rock, a boulder really, divided the lawn into two different countries. One half was brightly baked by the inescapable summer sun; the other half slept in the moody, perpetual half light cast by the rock over a groomed but scrubby terrain. Like many of the creatures that lived in the yard, Dilly regularly made a nest of the rock. Curled up inside a deep, protected cavity carved by time on one face, she'd sit as still as an icon in a sinner's grotto and watch the light shift time's shape. Occasionally, she'd flick an ant off her leg.

Or crush it with her innocent thumb.

Occasionally, she'd disappear into the rock. When the vanishings happened to her, Dilly couldn't tell you where she went. How. Or, possibly, who took her.

If she could tell you now, she'd explain those weren't important questions.

After all, the coming cataclysm had already begun.

*   *   *

Geologists called the rock in Dilly's backyard an "erratic."

Majestic and alone, the boulder had been set adrift on the landscape long ago by prehistoric glacial movement, a time when there were no suburbs, states, or picket fences. No people. No malls. No string cheese.

The rusted, ferrous veins in the gray limestone erratic intrigued geologists at the nearby university. After a photograph of it appeared in the newspaper, a graduate student and his professor began to drop by without warning, jotting observations in small notebooks they always kept on hand as if they expected the erratic to start moving again, to suddenly resume the path it had started millennia before.

Its composition and placement was "unusual," the geologists told her mother. The faded professor wiped the sweat from his brow, then dabbed at the bald patch under his hat. He gestured toward the slouching student beside him. "We'd like access if you don't mind."

Dilly wasn't sure what that meant exactly. But guessed her mother would no longer petition her father to have the rock removed from the yard. In the past, her mother complained the erratic gave off too much shade. That it encouraged moss to encroach on the lawn. To infiltrate the flower beds. The erratic blocked the view of their neighbor's potted gardenias, the distant copse of saplings by the silty, man-made pond.

"What kind of people," her mother once grumbled, "showcase a boulder in their backyard?" She was convinced it put off the neighbors.

But an "erratic"? That was a different story. Her mother could make that work.

At first, Dilly was pleased by her mother's shift in consciousness. Then the bearded graduate student turned up in their yard Saturday afternoon and took Dilly's spot in the nook.

"Hey." She kicked his dusty steel-tipped boot.

His eyes were closed. He didn't open them.

"You're in my rock."

He peeked a look at her. "Your rock?"

"My yard."

"Ah." He closed his eyes again. His fingers drummed on the notepad.

"What are you doing?" Dilly knew she sounded annoyed. Rude even.

The graduate student uncrossed his calloused knees. "Listening."

Dilly leaned against the rock. She didn't need to listen. She knew what he was hearing. She often heard the voices when she sat inside the rock too.

"What are they saying today?" she asked.

He looked surprised.

Dilly just shrugged. "It's my rock," she said again.

The grad student closed his eyes, concentrated. "They're saying, 'It's much much too late'."

Dilly nodded. "They've been saying that for a while now."

"And you haven't told anyone?" He studied her.

She kicked his boot again. She didn't want to call him stupid. Her mother would be mad.

"It's a rock," she said.

He cleared his throat and sat up, relinquishing the nook back to her. Dilly scrabbled in and curled up, her knees tight to her chest.

He leaned in close to her. Too close, she thought.

"I think it's best," he said, "if we keep this to ourselves."

Dilly just stared as he walked away, taking the scent of wet cardboard with him.

Idiot.

At least she didn't say it out loud.

*   *   *

At rest in her nook, Dilly couldn't be seen from the house. When she grew hungry, she clambered out from the rock, returned to her parents and their aromatic, well-lit rooms, their sandwich-shaped love. Waiting for her at the kitchen table she'd find a folded napkin by a plastic plate. A cup of milk on the right. A fork on the left. Her meal islanded as geometric food groups. At the sink, her mother washed dishes. In the next room, her father sat a penitent vigil before a humming TV.

Occasionally, her father joked that she'd turned "feral," especially on rainy days when Dilly returned from the erratic caked in a hieroglyphic spatter of mud and leaves. Dilly knew she was the changeling in her parents' home. That she preferred out over in, rock over kitchen. And in the stories her mother read at night, a changeling had to be tamed. Returned to its wilding home. Or put down.

Already, Dilly knew she was a girl who didn't belong.

At least in the erratic, she wasn't in error. Her compact child's body fit as neatly inside the rock as a rat in its burrow. In the erratic, Dilly found a place that felt safe. The rock eased her fears. Soothed her with its constancy. Its insistent, unvaried, if paradoxical, message.

Change, it said, *was coming*.

Sometimes she wished it would say more.

Be patient, it added.

Change would come for her. For her family. Much as it had come for the erratic before it was called an erratic: when it once was just an outcrop of mountain bound to other outcrops of mountain. Before it had been torn away from other rocks like itself. Then transformed into a "hardscape feature" in Dilly's backyard, domesticated with raised beds of mulch, oversized phlox, and pachysandra.

Change would come, it promised, for the child who crawled into its belly. And stayed there.

*   *   *

The next morning, the graduate student returned. When Dilly wandered outside with a breakfast bowl of toasted oats, she found him on his back half tucked into the stone, his legs dangling out of the erratic as he probed its interior, carefully scraping its private walls with his tiny chisel. In his free hand, he held a small recording device. In between probes, he held the recorder up toward the stone.

He was, she guessed, trying to capture the sounds of the erratic's voice.

"Won't do any good," she said.

He craned his neck up and squinted at her.

"I tried a long time ago," she said. "No luck."

The grad student slid out and crouched on his haunches. Dilly at once took his spot in the nook.

"Damn." He looked frustrated. "What else has it told you?"

Dilly looked at him and shrugged. "It's a rock. It's not complicated. *Change comes for us all.* Stuff like that."

The student nodded and shuffled his feet.

"We really should move it to the lab." He made a quick note to himself.

In the distance, Dilly could hear her mother chatting on the phone with one of the neighbors, something about getting the carpets washed. Or maybe the car detailed. The erratic had begun mumbling at her, but the geologist didn't notice.

Lost in thought, he started walking away.

When the graduate student looked back, Dilly was gone.

She was a kid. He didn't think anything of it.

*   *   *

Where did Dilly go?

Ask the question a different way.

Where *didn't* Dilly go?

Backyards of houses are home to savagery. Whether in sun or in shade, unseen arthropod barbarity wars its blue blood in the grass. In the trees above, birdsongs clash over egg-spattered nests. In the worlds between, mammals and humans show their fangs and teeth, fists and bombs, the violence swelling, erupting, receding: a predictable tide on land, air, and sea. Centipedes inject their venom. Spiders liquefy their prey. Raccoons steal eggs. Cats pounce on rabbits. Humans pummel and punch their young and make up later with gifts of stuffies or bowls of carmeled corn.

The erratic told her what to look for and what was to come: *Look.*

—To the rear of her home, a dark house. Breakfast dishes with bits of sliced pig abandoned on a counter. Ants harvesting toast crumbs. In the yard, a cat pulling apart a stunned mouse in the brittle undercarriage of a bush.

—To the right, at a desk by a window, a boy named Donny. One finger swiping naked girls on his tablet. The other, rummaging around in his lap. Sometimes digging into his nose.

Look.

—Next door, the quiet neighbor who gardened. Who tended

wild flowers while her husband worked. Writing a check to a children's fund. Rubbing a purpled bruise on her arm.

See the cataclysm that would soon rock her home, her neighborhood, the country, their planet. The drought that would one day parch Willow Park Lane. The rusted particulate air much too gritty to breathe.

The erratic knew what would happen while Dilly listened and watched. Soon, her limbs would go limp, her breath run shallow. Her skin would oxidize. Then splinter. Her bones would clast.

In no time at all, Dilly wouldn't even feel the limestone's chill.

*   *   *

Dilly wasn't thinking about the future the day she almost disappeared for good. Sitting by a nearby woodpile, looking for bugs beneath peeling reams of papered bark, she watched the grad student turn to wave to her. When he didn't see her, he dropped his hand in confusion, shrugged, kicked a stone, and walked off.

It should have been easy to see a girl in a bright purple coat against a stack of moldering logs.

Dilly followed the student quietly as he walked toward her neighbor's house, down the side path between their homes, and passed a crow perched in a thicket of berries, a small toad, lately dead, in its beak. The student rubbed his eyes, then stopped to admire a silent Mercedes parked outside the neighbor's garage. The unexpected driver was in the bedroom; the shade was up. The grad student's gaze turned to the window. So Dilly's gaze turned there too.

Finally, the student noticed her. And put a finger to his lips.

Inside the house, the neighbors were "going at it," as her father would say. Dilly was eight, or possibly twelve, maybe just ten years old. But she knew she was seeing trouble. "Going at it," meant a twisted arm, bruises, pulled hair for her neighbor. Even outside in the yard, Dilly could tell something was wrong. She knew what the erratic would say.

Change is coming.

Dilly looked at the grad student. He was shuffling his feet, he was turning away. Without looking at her, he walked quickly toward his car.

A rock can succumb to gravity. To the intensity of pressures around it.

Dilly picked up a rock, gauged its weight. As soon as she launched it at the window, she ran. When the glass cracked, the grad student looked back. Then hastily got into his car.

Above them on Willow Park Lane, the sun, also a rock, was undergoing constant incandescent transformation. Safe in the erratic, Dilly held her hand up as she heard doors slam. Then muted shouts. Farther off, the sound of the grad student's punctured muffler rumbling exhausted carbolic life as he drove the Chevy down the street.

Silhouetted above her head, Dilly's palm glowed, her inner fire shining through. She was molten. Metamorphic.

Dilly understood what the grad student did not.

A rock can always be moved.

*   *   *

Two days later, Dilly emerged from the erratic. By then, her tongue had transformed into limestone. Sluggish and pale, she could barely talk.

Dazed, she wandered into the kitchen and fell into her mother's arms.

"You're hurting me." Dilly could barely understand her own voice. The pitch was deeper, more resonant, than she remembered. It reverberated: the sound of pipe on stone.

When her mother finally released her, Dilly tried to apologize—for disappearing, for not telling her mother about the erratic's strange message, for not being the daughter her parents wanted. But her mouth was full of gravel and her legs felt numb. When she collapsed, her mother went with her, panting and whining like a dog tending the runt of the litter. In her grunts, Dilly could hear concern. Resignation. Dismay.

Soon, Dilly was wrapped in a blanket, and tucked into her bed. A doctor stopped by and checked her in places she'd never been checked before. Not long after, there was a policeman. In the draped afternoon twilight, he took notes while her mother eavesdropped out in the hall. Dilly tried to explain that she'd been in the yard. That she'd just been upset; had fallen asleep in the rock.

That she hadn't gone anywhere at all.

She told the same story over and over. Her mother, the doctor, the policemen—they listened and nodded. But Dilly could tell they didn't believe her.

Didn't she know, her mother said, that the erratic was the first place they'd looked? Couldn't she remember where she'd really gone?

Her mother pulled the blanket up, tucked it around her. She hadn't done that since Dilly was seven, or maybe four, or possibly ten years old.

"I'm right here when you're ready," her mother said as she stood.

The absence she left in Dilly's bedroom was the dark matter formed by the smallest of planets after passing through a black hole.

*   *   *

For the first time, Dilly tried to tell her parents what the erratic was saying. But they hushed her. Kept her home from school. Soon, her mother began grousing about the erratic's influence over their family. This time, Dilly could tell her father was listening.

In the meantime, her mother kept pushing Dilly to tell the "real" story. The new family at the end of the street, she said: had they ever met? How about the family with the green ranch on the next block? They had a rough looking dog. A stepson in college. Had Dilly ever been invited inside?

For the next few weeks, Dilly tried to keep to herself. But her mother was never far out of earshot. And her father, now home on time each night, was suddenly interested in all her ideas. The conversations at the kitchen table were exhausting.

No wonder infants cry so much, Dilly thought. They must go mad from all the attention.

The erratic told her to be patient. Their attention would ease. *All things eventually ease*, it said. It was the nature of physics. Intensity cannot be maintained. Soon, even the universe would ease. Relent. Decay.

When the grad student knocked on their front door two days later, his hat in his hands, her mother stepped outside to talk with him. Dilly couldn't hear what he was saying, but the timbre of her mother's voice could have cut a tree in half.

Vaguely, Dilly felt sorry for them. The way a rock might feel sorry for the soft earth cradling its weight.

Free for the first time in days, Dilly quickly went outside and at once curled up in the stone.

There, as the erratic's voices swelled—*Look*, it muttered, *look!*—she couldn't hear the strangled sound of her mother's fear.

*   *   *

As the hours passed, then days, months, finally years, Dilly didn't disappear so much as become the rock in which she sat. The more she listened, the more she took on the rock's point of view. First a stillness. A slowness that was not slow because there was no other possible pace. A patience of thought that took the time required for each idea to fully form. A sense of time expanding. Of expansive time. Slowly, Dilly's pale skin hardened, was transversed by the deep red ferrous veins that the geologists once called "unexpected."

Dilly couldn't say when she realized the erratic wasn't really a stone at all, but a sedimented being composed of girls like her. Other children before her, and some long after, had (would) sit in the stone as Dilly had sat. They had (would) listen. They had (would) transform too.

Dilly couldn't say when her last disappearance began to happen. If it started years before, the very first time she sat in the rock. Or the last time, while her mother dispatched the geology student, then returned to the kitchen to find Dilly gone. Perhaps it only began as her mother called for her, a strange panicked bark that echoed down the street.

By the time her mother called the police and her father, by the time the detectives arrived to scout the yard for clues, Dilly knew change had come to her. That change was already under way. But that her change was not new.

That all stones, everywhere—*Look!*—were just girls waiting for the universe to complete its interminable work.

Volunteers arrived. Then left. The search began. Then ended.

Time passed.

More time passed.

In time, her family was gone.

And all memory of Dilly passed with them. Even Dilly's memory of herself as "Dilly" and not something that "once was Dilly but became something else" passed too. There was no Dilly to remember the Dilly who once believed she was Dilly.

There was only a large rock and the earth.

A girl is a porous compaction of subcutaneous layers.

The erratic had been a girl many times before.

Ghost

CB Anderson

Before the dog, in the aftermath of the move to Bay Haven, Roslyn Dubois found something like contentment—a steady state that arrived as the months became a year became three years in May. She inhabited the feeling gingerly, as if it were a tent she'd pitched without instructions. It was standing. It could fall.

In the mornings, she rose early to walk the development before it got hot. Twice a week she shopped at Groff's outdoor market, where they sold homemade butter and tropical jams. Sometimes she and Marcel invited couples they'd met at the AME church to dinner. On those evenings Marcel grilled chicken in the lanai adjacent to a small backyard in which he grew roses and, along the fence, a cascade of bougainvillea.

"Paradise," their new friend Norm Holden, a retired attorney like Marcel, called Bay Haven.

At sixty-eight, Marcel was robust in this new life a thousand miles from Baltimore, his Parkinson's agreeably in abeyance. He was open to everything: golf dates, street fairs, and, by night, outings to view constellations or to listen to the steel drum band on the beach. Roslyn went along, liked the evenings outdoors when the dark settled around her.

She understood this, that Marcel tended toward buoyancy and she toward its opposite. But somehow they balanced each other, they always had and more so now, when the retirement she'd worried about—*What would they do all day?*—took form propi-tiously, the world at once smaller in its demands and larger in its offerings. Who knew the satisfaction she'd derive from a chip shot on the Heritage Bay golf course? Who knew Marcel had a green thumb? Everything he brought home, even bedraggled snips on clearance at Home Depot, thrived when he put them in the ground.

All this before the dog. And then—June, a month into their fourth year in Florida, something about Marcel, excesses, an added exuberance, began to make her watchful. At first it wasn't much: five kinds of ice cream when she sent him out for vanilla to go with the cobbler she was making for dinner with the Holdens. Too-long absences when he was running errands. The morning not long ago when he'd come home with the news that he'd stopped to register for intensive Spanish at the community center. When she asked why, he said he wanted to be able to talk with their next-door neighbors.

Roslyn thought it enough to nod when she and Marcel pulled into the driveway as the new neighbors were backing down theirs. In truth, she was put off by them—by the kids diving into her shrubs to retrieve balls and by the cars that pulled up on week-end afternoons to disgorge families with armfuls of Tupperware for barbecues that went late into the night. The neighbors' fun seemed so large and effortless. Roslyn lay in bed listening to the merrymaking, wishing it would end. How did they find so much to laugh about?

*   *   *

Marcel's class disrupted their golf schedule. In the mornings while he was gone, Roslyn started going to the pool, arriving home itch-ing from chlorine and overfilled with gossip. As they ate lunch, she gave updates she didn't really care about—the Carvers' addition, the Lewis' three weeks in Vermont—and he offered up phrases in Spanish. "Aqui tienes," he'd say as he poured her sweet tea. "Salud!" Roslyn rolled her eyes, but the Latin exuberance suited him.

One night when she was almost asleep, Marcel turned to her in bed. "Remember that story I showed you about greyhounds, how tracks all over the country are closing?"

Eyes still closed, Roslyn murmured assent. Marcel went on:

greyhound rescues were overrun. The shelter on the edge of Bay Haven, for instance—two hundred dogs in a space designed for fifty. And, well, Marcel wanted them to adopt one. He'd seen him—*Him?* Roslyn was fully awake now—when he drove out there on Thursday. "They're sweet dogs, Roz," he said. "I think we should help."

His eyes were on hers when she opened them. She sat up against the headboard. She didn't like dogs or pets of any sort. He knew that. But as easy as it had been for her to raise their daughter and son with the discipline Marcel seemed reluctant to dispense, it had always been hard for her to deny *him*. Time and again she'd acquiesced because for forty years saying yes generally had led to something good. He'd been the one to push for Florida and for this small, fine house that exceeded their price range but turned out to be right.

And before that, in Baltimore when the kids were young: the backyard trampoline, the Christmas movie marathons that went past midnight. Or the Polar Caves, a spur-of-the-moment trip to Pennsylvania that Marcel had talked her into one hot summer weekend. At the entrance, they'd been given flashlights and allowed to roam. Roslyn still remembered Dominique and Will in the chilly gloom, faces lit as they rounded a corner. "I *love* this," Will had said. And if Roslyn couldn't inhabit the moment the way Marcel and the kids could, it had been enough to sense her son's delight.

In doing so she'd outdistanced her own mother, who'd managed to raise Roslyn but not to enjoy her. It was Marcel who'd provided her with an exit from the dingy walk-up when she was nineteen, a secretarial student at Baltimore State. He played guard for BSU basketball and lived off campus with his family. Sitting at games with them, three sisters and parents who reveled in their children in a way Roslyn never would have thought possible, she felt peaceably subsumed.

So, heaven help them, there she and Marcel were at the greyhound shelter on a Monday afternoon. Inside the cinderblock building, dogs were everywhere, stacked three-high in metal crates. The smells layered disinfectant, urine, and something vaguely meaty. It was quieter than Roslyn would have expected. The dog Marcel wanted occupied a midlevel crate halfway down a hall. Skinny, a silvery no-color. Deep, bony chest. At their approach, he pressed his nose through the wire mesh. Roslyn shivered in the over-chilled air. "He's kind of ugly."

Marcel laughed. "Well. He has beautiful eyes."

Roslyn pulled herself closer inside her sweater. "He looks like a ghost."

Another laugh. "I see what you mean."

Hence the greyhound's new name, only—irritatingly—in Spanish: Fantasmo on the purple tag Marcel had engraved the next morning at PetSmart. Already he and the dog were a pair, heading off together after breakfast and returning with a half-dozen bags and a large, plushy bed that the dog lowered himself into, limb by limb, as soon as Marcel set it beside the couch.

"Not there," said Roslyn, toeing the edge of the bed, also purple, her favorite color although the room was done in neutrals. "It doesn't go with the sofa. And I don't want him stinking up the living room."

"He shouldn't stink anymore. They groomed him. Now he smells like coconut, don't you, Fan?"

The dog looked up at him with something like a smile. When Marcel pushed open the slider to go water the roses, Fantasmo rose, creakily, to follow. "He is nine," said Marcel. "I got fish oil for his arthritis." Upright, the dog moved fluidly past Roslyn and out the door with Marcel, into the midday sun.

*   *   *

Two weeks later, a Tuesday, Roslyn came home from the pool to find Marcel returned from his class and gone again, having taken the dog with him. She made lunch, waited, was fretting over the pan of congealing egg noodles when the phone rang.

She picked up before the second ring. "Where are you?"

"At work," Will said. A pause. "You all right, Mama?"

"Of course." She forced a lighter tone. Will, attuned to everything, inclined, like her, to somberness. She needed, still—always—to model her most cheerful self. "Dad's late for lunch is all."

"I was thinking of coming down early. Maybe in a couple of weeks?"

"Wonderful," said Roslyn, and it was—she enjoyed visits from the kids, was gratified that they liked Bay Haven. Dominique, when she and Darius visited from New York, went on about the mangrove tunnels on the bit of beach to which their deed granted access. Even Will, though he wasn't outdoorsy like Dominique, settled into the guest room without complaint for a week each December and May.

"I need to get away," he was saying. "It's so dark up here. And cold, already."

"Oh, I remember." Her cell vibrated on the counter. "Come anytime you want, Willie. Dom and Darius won't be here until January." The cell kept buzzing. "Dad's calling—I should probably get it."

But it was Norm Holden. "Roz? Marcel took my boat out." Norm's voice was loud through the speaker, accusatory. "Do you know what he's doing?"

Roslyn left the front door unlatched, the skin on her insteps blistering as she half-ran to the bay in sandals. By the time she got there, a few neighbors had gathered. Norm was peering into his binoculars, reporting: "Looks like he's just floating with the engine cut. I think he's got a dog with him, a big one." He put the binoculars down, saw her. "Where'd he get a dog?"

Three things occurred to Roslyn: that it had been a month since they'd seen the Holdens, that Marcel must have swum out to the boat because the dinghy wasn't on the mooring, that somehow she should have foreseen this. The sun drilled down, hotter than October had a right to be. Everyone was watching. She fought an impulse to sink onto the stony beach. Georgia Holden took her arm. "He probably left a message that he was taking it out," she said. "He knows the keys are in it."

When Roslyn didn't reply, Georgia turned her back on the others, lowered her voice. "This is not like Marcel." It was true, or would have been, until recently. Roslyn was awash in unreality, dislocated; she did not recognize this moment, the day, as possibly belonging to her life. The prayer she attempted would not take form. For what should she be asking? Pressure built behind her eyes as she leaned into Georgia's perfumed embrace, also unfamiliar, spicier than her usual blend of talcum and coconut. She wiped her eyes, took off her sandals and waded into the water with Georgia at her side. The salt stung her feet in a way that she welcomed.

The boat motor rumbled, then ratcheted up. "He's coming in," Norm said, unnecessarily, because Marcel was gunning for the beach, bearing down on them in such a way that when he hooked a sudden left and slowed, the wake washed over her and Georgia. They were soaked to their hips. Georgia turned for the shore. "He didn't need to do that," she said.

Norm was holding the bow of the boat. "Could you please go get the dinghy, Georgia?" he asked, his voice tighter than Roslyn had ever heard it. He didn't look at Marcel. The neighbors had disappeared when Marcel came in, as if observing the convention that calls for passersby to look away from a crash.

Marcel leaned down toward Norm. "Sorry. I got caught up in the beautiful day. I know I should have checked in with you."

Norm did not respond. In the silence, Marcel shifted his focus to Roslyn.

"He can swim," he said.

"Who can?"

"Fan can. I told him to stay on the beach and I'd come back for him, but he followed me. Greyhounds aren't supposed to know how to swim." He thumped the dog with affection, seemingly unfazed by Norm's stoniness or the commotion he'd caused. "He really is amazing."

"What's the matter with you?" Roslyn was crying for real now, didn't care that Norm was standing there. "You took Norm's boat without asking. You embarrassed us. Shut up about the dog."

Hurt blanketed Marcel's face. He stared out at the water, then picked up the greyhound and climbed down the ladder. The stones were sharp, and Marcel was barefoot, but he didn't seem to notice as he walked with the animal in his arms up the beach and into the mangroves.

*   *   *

They were in the backyard amid a riot of second-bloom roses, the most exuberant since Marcel had planted them. Marcel was re-gluing the legs on an old chair. Roslyn sat with her back to him, working her way through the *Haven Times*.

"We should invite Cora down this winter," he said. In the three days since the boat, they'd barely spoken, and when they did it was this: pontiff-like issuances from Marcel that she ignored.

"You should get ready for your appointment," she told him.

"It's been too long since we've seen her." A thud as he set the chair down. "You might even have fun."

Roslyn was conceding nothing, especially today, especially on the topic of her mother, who'd been lukewarm at best. Cora had provided secondhand clothing, food from cans, and not much else. When Roslyn started going to Marcel's house, she'd been stunned by the plenitude. Mrs. Dubois' Creole meals at the long oak table, rounds of school and sports events, Bible study every Wednesday night: the Dubois household offered a window on the celebration of dailiness.

The mid-morning sun was inching up Roslyn's legs. She tucked them beneath her. She'd heard enough AME sermons to at least approximate forgiveness of her mother. *Cora is not the issue. You are*, she started to say, but something about Marcel's face, an echo of the hurt from the boat, stopped her.

Yesterday he'd gone the few doors down to the Holdens' with a new putter for Norm to try to patch things up. Roslyn had heard laughter, so apparently it had gone well. Maybe the boat was a one-off. Maybe she'd overreacted. Marcel was a good man, caring. He remembered people's anniversaries and birthdays. Every morning he made coffee and brought it to her in bed. When she kicked off her shoes at night, he aligned them in the closet alongside his in tidy rows. She glanced at the greyhound, hunkered in the scant shade of the bougainvillea. At least he didn't bark.

The quiet returned, easier than before. In her mind Roslyn was walking the oiled floors of Groff's, assembling things for the dinner she would make: pork chops, dirty rice, some brussels sprouts in olive oil. She rose from her chair, reached for scissors and gloves from Marcel's toolbox to snip a few roses. Yellow blooms, pink, blood red—perfect. They accumulated in her hand, the yellow ones rimmed with burgundy. Key lime pie for dessert.

*   *   *

"It's probably the L-dopa." Post-examination, Marcel and Martin were sitting in Martin's office, where Roslyn had joined them.

"What is?"

"The lability. The increased impulsivity you've described. And today Marcel told me he's been punding."

"Punding?"

"Arranging things. The items in a billfold, say, or glasses in the cupboard, repeatedly."

So far Marcel had said nothing. Roslyn looked at him. He held her gaze—*You're the one who made me come*—but did not speak. She thought of their shoes, so neat in the closet. Marcel replaced whichever ones she was wearing the moment she took them off. How long had he been doing that?

Suddenly, intensely, she wished they'd stayed home. A humming started in her ears. Martin leaned forward in his chair, Marcel sat back, a leaf from the fig tree by the window fluttered to the floor. "—all the clinical signs," Martin was saying. He looked over at Marcel. "As I said, it's either over-response or misuse. Either way, we should bring you in for a week and taper it down."

Bring him in? Misuse? Roslyn's heart thudded in her throat. "You mean abusing the L-dopa?"

Marcel stood, headed for the door.

"I'm not saying that." Martin frowned, sighed. "I'm sorry. What I mean is, there's too much in your system. It's not safe."

Marcel opened the door, stood there filling the frame. "I'm not coming in," he said. "We should go, Roz."

Outside it was pouring. Roslyn ran for the car, rain drenching her blouse as Marcel fumbled for the keys. Martin had been Marcel's neurologist since they'd moved to Florida, and they'd left his office without a word.

Marcel drove slowly in the downpour. Al Green was coming through the speakers—"To Sir With Love." Roslyn switched off the CD player. They were back to heavy silence, long empty minutes during which she pressed the side of her head against the window. Florida still seemed foreign during thunderstorms, a place capable of fury. The edges of the road were slick with oil and dirty foam. Wind buffeted the car.

When Marcel pulled into the Checkers, she sat up. "No," she said, but couldn't find it in herself to direct him elsewhere. Her head ached, and her wet blouse clung to her skin. She didn't feel like shopping anymore, couldn't remember the meal she'd planned.

"What's going on?" she said.

"I thought we'd get burgers."

"Marcel."

He fiddled with the AC. "You know what's going on."

"I don't."

"You do. You've seen it getting worse." He turned in his seat, regarded her gently. "Roz. You know I've been taking more."

She didn't know. She did. Marcel lifted his left pant leg to show the brace, held out his hands. Relentlessly they trembled, the way they had before the L-dopa.

"But you can't keep taking more."

"I can." Marcel looked at his hands, quivering as if not part of him. "It helps."

"You need to do what Martin says."

Marcel shook his head, set his mouth in what she recognized as *conversation over*. He shifted into drive, pulled back onto Palmetto Road. Away from the neon hues of the Checkers lot, his face was drained of color.

Roslyn kept pressing. "Will's coming in ten days," she said. "And Dominique after that. What if something like Norm's boat happens again?"

"It won't."

Now it was her turn to be gentle. "It could," she said. "You don't know. Did you plan for the boat to go that way?"

Rain pounded on the roof, and lightning struck not far away. Marcel's face barely loosened. "I didn't have a plan," he said.

*   *   *

They didn't like each other much, she and the dog. Roslyn refused to call him by his Spanish name, and he refused the food she set out. Two days into Marcel's stay at Central, the dog still hadn't touched the fancy kibble from the bag with wolves on the front.

On Wednesday she brought him outside, seven a.m. for her walk—now his walk too—was clipping on his leash when one of the boys from next door came out from behind the fence. Roslyn would have been startled, but she'd heard him whistling, the long thin notes of someone who's learning. Ghost looked up with interest.

"Hey, Fantasmo," the boy said. So Marcel had introduced them. The boy was alone, no brothers or parents in sight. He walked along with her, kept whistling a staccato one-note, something less than a birdcall.

"No school today?" Roslyn asked.

"Vacation. My mom's taking us to the batting cage." He reached down, petted Ghost's head. The dog drew back his lips in his ghastly smile. "He doesn't bite," the boy said, as if to reassure himself.

They were at the corner where Roslyn usually turned toward the canal. "Your parents will be worried," she said by way of suggesting he go back.

The boy shook his head. "Still asleep." Even so, she changed her route, turned around and walked the street instead, back and forth in the strengthening light in case his parents came looking. No one else was out. Norm and Georgia's house, shutters closed, was a blank face staring out at the street. When she'd told Georgia about Marcel's hospitalization, Georgia had been kind but reserved. Roslyn recognized it as the way retirees in Florida handled other people's illnesses: an acquired remove. Too many people got sick, got sicker, died. You could only afford to get so close.

They walked like this, an occasional whistle, the jingle of Ghost's tags, a shred of conversation. The boy's name was Daniel. Up the street and back, up and back, the sun growing hot on Roslyn's uncovered head. She didn't blame Georgia. People got thick-skinned to protect themselves from the dampening effects of misfortune.

When Roslyn finally stopped, the dog pulled on his leash toward Daniel, as if hoping to continue his day with him rather than with her. The boy ran his hand down Ghost's side, and the dog leaned against him.

"He's so skinny," Daniel said.

"He is. And now he's not eating." She didn't want to care, but she did.

The boy started whistling again, the notes stronger now that he'd practiced, and Roslyn waited for him to turn away. Before he did, he peered up through a fringe of bangs.

"Give him something he likes, even if it's bad for him."

That seemed like sound advice. Inside, she pulled out a pan and laid it with bacon, added eggs—no spices—and cooked them easy over. She was making breakfast for a dog, all the sillier because when she divided it and slid his onto a plate, he sniffed at it, then sighed and walked away.

Later, when she and Marcel were sitting in the lounge at the end of his wing, she told him the dog wouldn't eat. "Dogs do that. He's probably wondering where I am," Marcel said. His voice was weaker, tremulous. He'd seemed unsteady getting to the lounge. Clearly the L-dopa had dropped.

Roslyn sipped her tea, took a breath. Marcel reached for her hand, enfolded it in his trembling one. "You can see the level's down," he said. "Good, I guess, for me getting out of here." But because his liver enzymes were up, Martin would not prescribe more L-dopa. "He'll try something else, although he says we can't look for the same response."

Part of her had expected this, but Marcel pressed on in his newly quiet voice. "We should be thinking long-term." He tightened his grip on her hand. "I've looked at a few assisted living places. Some are really nice."

Roslyn stared at him. Yet another thing he'd done on his own during his outings. Marcel was, she saw, more than just impulsive—he was self-reliant.

He should have known to stop, but he kept on: "They seem almost like resorts—pools and yoga classes, things like that. You could join me when you're ready."

Roslyn lifted her tea, cold, then set it down hard. "Just like that," she said. "It's clear you've done a lot of thinking."

"I'm okay with it, I am. I knew upping the L-dopa might not do it."

"I am not okay." Roslyn pulled her hand from his hand and stood. "I have to go take care of things."

At home, the eggs and bacon still sat in Ghost's bowl. Roslyn pulled out a steak. In the lanai, she started the grill and laid the meat over the fire. While it was cooking, she went outside, picked up the hose. Marcel's roses were dry. She let a thin stream of water wash over their roots, careful not to splash the leaves. It was nintey degrees, still unseasonable, the sun heavy overhead.

Inside, she began pulling shades on the south and west sides of the house. As she was finishing up, the doorbell rang. She found the dog by her side when she went to the foyer.

It was the boy from next door. "Hi," Roslyn said. She fished for his name. "Daniel."

He regarded her seriously. "I brought this for Fantasmo." In his hand was what looked like a bar of candy. "Maybe he will like it."

"Thank you," Roslyn said. "That was nice of you." After she'd closed the door, she sat down on the sofa and inspected the wrapper. KitKat. Wasn't chocolate bad for dogs? She unwrapped it, broke off a stick. The sweetness filled her mouth. She let it stay there a while, chewed and swallowed then broke off another wafer until all four were gone. The dog fixed his eyes on hers.

"Not good for you." She patted the top of his head—softer than she'd imagined.

There was smoke and the smell of something charred. When she lifted the lid of the grill the steak was black, inedible. Roslyn snapped off the burners. Back on the sofa she put her head in her hands, felt a great blank emptiness that frightened her. So much could happen. So much remained unknown. She got up, made her way to the bedroom and lay down. The chocolate was leaden in her belly. She thought she might be sick, but after a few minutes the feeling subsided.

It was only four p.m., but the day felt done. In the closet, Roslyn pulled off her dress and reached for a robe. Her slippers, leather mules that Marcel had gotten for her birthday, were in the middle of the rows he'd made. She picked up the slippers, put them on. If you counted the hole they left, there were twelve pairs side by side in each of three rows, plus the flats she'd worn earlier that day. Seventy-four shoes altogether. She and Marcel would never wear them out. Roslyn nudged the flats with her toe, kicked them, kept kicking until the rows were wrecked then sat on the floor and wept. The marks on the wall were permanent.

*   *   *

Ghost disappeared on Friday, an hour before she was supposed to pick up Marcel. One minute the dog was with her at the end of the street. The next he was bounding into the wooded area behind the last house.

She chased him, but after fifty yards she had to stop. Blood trickled down one of her shins—she'd struck it on something, a rock or a log—and a bruise was rising.

Vines and brush grew thick, and a ravine led down to a creek she hadn't known was there. The dog was nowhere in sight. Apart from cicadas and the distant hum of traffic, it was quiet. "Ghost," she called, "Come, Ghost" and then, "Come, Fantasmo!" She stood still and listened, nothing, worried about his leash getting caught on a branch. About snakes or alligators near the water. Why had she set down the leash when she tied her shoe?

The woods extended back to a large parcel that had been abandoned mid-development, the houses half-built shells. A dog could run a mile deep without anyone seeing him. "Fantasmo," she shouted. "Come!"

"Roz? Are you okay in there?" She turned. Norm, who'd been out trimming his hedges, stood at the verge.

"I've lost the dog," she said when she'd walked back to him. "And I'm late to pick up Marcel at the hospital."

Then Georgia was there too, and it was somehow agreed that they'd go for Marcel while Roslyn stayed. Roslyn wasn't sure it was right, wasn't sure what was right, but she let them go and returned to the woods. Anger eddied around her. The forces that had led her here seemed senseless. She thought about how she'd look in church on Sunday, welts from mosquito bites, a large egg on her shin. Why even bother going?

Roslyn called the dog, shouted, walked in a small circle. The sun dropped behind the trees, and the gathering shade drew more mosquitos. The heat held on.

Finally it was Marcel who stood at the edge of the woods where Norm had earlier. Roslyn went to him, over the path she'd worn clear, leaned into his embrace. She could sense he didn't blame her.

"He just ran," she said.

Marcel rubbed her back. "Go home and take care of your leg. Go on. I'll stay here."

Roslyn was tired. She shook her head but turned anyway toward the house. It seemed a long way off. Halfway there she paused to rest, which is when she saw Ghost, a silver blur that raced to Marcel, jumped up on him in greeting, then continued to her and stopped. He was panting. His eyes shone. Roslyn reached down and picked up the leash.

Inside, the dog went straight to his kibble, head in bowl until it was gone. Marcel came in, stood watching beside her. She felt cautiousness between them, a sense of all that was at stake. It was a daily act of will to turn toward the other. She was just now aware of it.

"I deadheaded your roses," Roslyn told him. "And cleaned the steak off the grill."

"I feel like a swim," Marcel said. "Do you want to join me?"

Roslyn didn't, but she went into the bedroom and put on her suit. As she was pulling towels from the closet, Ghost showed up at her side. Marcel raised his eyebrows. "He can come," she said.

At the pool, she and Marcel were careful with each other. "Excuse me," Roslyn said when she bumped him while side-stroking. Marcel smiled and moved aside. Ghost looked on from the edge.

Then, when she had finished her laps, as the last of the light was leaving the pool, Marcel splashed her and she splashed back—they'd used to love to swim together. He got out to plunge from the edge, a flop of a dive that made her laugh. When he resurfaced, he shook water from his hair and grinned. Slowly the water settled.

Roslyn turned on her back, floated. Westering sun, a rising moon. If she took a big enough breath, she didn't need to move to stay afloat. Water filled her ears. Will was coming in a week, she realized, and she was not yet ready.

A Creature Comes Home

H. L. Nelson

Man is the only creature that refuses to be what he is.
—Albert Camus

The animal edges toward the fence in the subfuscous evening light. It's a good hundred feet from the porch, but Cahill, watching from his father's stool, can tell it's solidly built and sized like an alpha, much larger than the wolfdogs that live here on his father's property. Its head is as tall as his own hips, and muscle ropes from shoulders to haunches, overlaid with two coats of thick black fur. Cahill senses it can jump the fence if it wants to, but is waiting for him to let it in. He blows smoke at the piercing winter air, wondering if he has enough room for the animal and how long it might hulk there if he does nothing. Ardy, Cahill's father, would have let the animal right in if he wasn't currently missing. Ardy Womack didn't fear much of anything.

That settles the matter.

Cahill rises from his stool and clumps down his father's peeling porch steps, grinds the butt of his Marlboro into the rich vertisol, and flicks it into a halved ginger ale can. He opens the first gate of the double-gated, twenty-foot run, which marks the entrance to the wolfdog sanctuary, hoping the animal goes in easily. His plan is to leave it in there for a bit until he can see how the others get along with it through the 9-gauge chain link. It could be the alpha of the pack, newly returned, or not—he'd soon see.

As he strides toward the main gate, the dark animal lifts its head and sniffs several times in his direction, then lowers it and tentatively trembles its tail in greeting. It doesn't have the same hybrid look as the others; its ears are smaller and fully furred inside, and its eyes are almond-shaped, darkly lined, and golden. Cahill decides he doesn't much like the look of it.

When he opens the hasp and the large gate, careful to keep the metal between his body and the canine, he expects it to wait a while before slinking in. Instead, it charges in full speed, much faster and sleeker than he thought it capable. His breath catches in his throat and he wonders if it's his time. The animal comes to a fluid stop inside the run, turns, and lies down. It puts its head on its paws and stares at Cahill. He's uneasy, but at least the thing is in the run. It doesn't move when he closes the first gate, locking it in.

Cahill keeps the inside lights off as he slumps in his father's cracked leather club chair, the biggest supermoon of the year rising over the backyard, red-orange and round as a summer squash. Everything under it seems swabbed in iodine, including the animal that watches him through the large sunroom windows. Its eyes shine golden red from the umber rust of its coat. He guzzles a ginger ale. He gave up drinking after Linda left him, the two of them drifting from each other like separated landmasses, his drinking the acting faultline. It was the way Cahill had known to numb himself. He doesn't like to think about that stretch of time after Linda left.

Needing more ginger ale, he heads to the fridge through the hall, passing the maple staircase his grandfather had made. It leads upstairs to a small dusty room plus small attic space that he put his claim on when he was a defiant teen in the 80s, going head to head with his father. Ardy was a hardened ex-Marine who expected everyone to fall in line in his house. In Cahill's mind, his father didn't approve of anything the young Cahill did or wanted to do. He flew off the handle when Cahill didn't keep his word, badgered him constantly to "cut his goddamn hippie hair," and once when Cahill was fourteen, Ardy made him trudge three miles in 102-degree weather carrying a forty pound boulder. All because he forgot to mow a strip of grass on the side of the house.

In the kitchen, he pulls the drink and sandwich makings out of the fridge and places them on the butcher block countertop, full of nicks and grooves from Ardy and Cahill's inattentive food fumblings after Cahill's mother, Judith, became bedridden. She had always used a cutting board on top of it, yet he and his father hadn't. After her death, Ardy seemed not to know how to care for himself. The house, in a way, still felt like a brooding old man.

Taking his sandwich back to the sunroom, Cahill sits heavily in the club chair. The animal still watches him through the window. He goes over what he knows about his father's disappearance: three months before, the veterans who would come by Ardy's sanctuary for their twice weekly Wolves and Warriors therapy session found the place bereft. They got in touch with the local sheriff's office, who got in touch with Ardy's only living sister, Westa, and let her know Ardy was missing.

His Aunt Westa, who he'd been closer to than his father, called him and he was unexpectedly happy to hear her familiar voice. "I know you haven't talked to your Pa in decades, but this is still gonna come as a shock." He heard her take a draw on a Newport— same old pack-a-day Aunt Westa. "Ardy up and left in his truck. No one knows where he is. The sheriff poked around his property, and I think that lazy sunofabitch won't do anything more. There're all these damn wolfdogs on the property and I don't know what to do with 'em. There were a few idiots in the area who got wolves from up north and were breeding 'em with local dogs, then got surprised when the damn things ate their chickens or killed other livestock, so Ardy took 'em in. I told him it wasn't a good idea, but he made a go of it. And now he's just gone. I'm sorry, honey."

Cahill didn't know what to think. He told his aunt he'd come up to visit the next weekend and see what could be done. The Ardy Womack of twenty-five years ago wasn't one to walk out on his responsibilities. Neither was he one to make a wolfdog sanctuary and host therapy classes for military vets. Cahill understood that people could change, but his father didn't fall into that group. He would always be a judgmental hard-ass. Cahill was sure his father would turn up, and would ask them why the hell they were so damn worried, acting like it was their fault he'd gone missing.

The weather that next weekend when he drove to his aunt's was just past the oppressive suffocation of summer. Cahill had felt a clean sharpness high in his nose, a tinge of pure, cold air and remembered how much he loved this time of year back home. He drove with the windows down and listened to the buzz and click of cicadas in the fields off the side of the road.

Westa greeted him in front of her 70s-style ranch with a jowly kiss. She beamed up at him, looking fat and sassy—just as he remembered her. "Well, bless my buttered rolls but if you don't look like your Mama, God rest her soul." She glanced up at the sky as if conferring with his mother, then clapped him on the arm and said, "My heavens, but we have some catching up to do!" She threaded her arm through his, and ushered him into her sunny kitchen for a beef chili and toast lunch.

After, they headed out to the property he grew up on. When he saw the old house as they bumped over the drive, curving round a stand of burr oaks in the large front yard, a pang of melancholy that he didn't understand bounced around inside him like the baseball he used to ricochet off the siding after his cousins went home when summer was over.

The family home had changed some, mostly the wolfdog pens, the ten-foot fence and double gates, and of course the dogs themselves. There were eight of them. Cahill didn't know anything about wolves, but he knew quite a bit about dogs and could tell when he and Westa got closer that they were Malamutes, Huskies, and German Shepherds with varying degrees of wolf. Some had longer cow-hocked legs, thick dark nails, extended muzzles. They moved along the interior fenceline, ears alert, peering at him. When they switched their gaze to his aunt, they wagged their tails and moved toward their respective pens and food bowls. They watched Cahill through the chain link as they gorged on the cuts of raw, half-frozen meat he and Westa had found in Ardy's deep freeze, and he wondered what in the world had driven his father to create a home for such creatures.

After talking to Westa all that day and into the evening, he mulled over moving home for a time, to take care of the dogs and the property just until his father returned. Pride and fear were making him reserved, but it felt like a stronger force was pulling him to his family's property. He and Ardy had a lot to work through, and yet neither had budged all those years, even when Linda left and Cahill felt like a small boy who just needed his father. He wished he'd been able to introduce Linda to Ardy so the old man would know that Cahill had at one point done something right.

He moved back home within the month. The first evening, by the light of his mother's favorite red antique kerosene lamp, he used the satellite Internet and old Dell to learn about the animals he'd become responsible for. He talked himself into riffling through his father's papers to see if there were any clues as to his whereabouts.

There was a stack of bills on top of the desk that showed hundreds of dollars of credit in each account; Ardy still insisted bills be paid ahead. Under them, Cahill found a small leather-bound ledger and flipped it open, expecting to see rows of figures. Instead, the word "Journal" was scrawled at the top of the first page, then further down was a lone entry:

March 23, 2003
I feel a kinship with these dogs. Don't quite understand it but whatever it is I hope it can help the other men. Many of them look happy when they're here. It's as if they can forget for a time about their battles—the ones they fought overseas and the ones they're still fighting. Sometimes it's one and the same.

Cahill flipped the page.

May 14, 2003
Man dropped by and offered to pay me $5000 cash for all the dogs. Real slimy, polyester suit. I said no of course. Probably wants to fight 'em. Pissed me off if you want to know the truth. I best not see him around here again.

He flipped ahead several pages.

September 22, 2010
Any of these vets who come here to spend time with the dogs could be me. Any of 'em. Hodge especially took his tour real hard, what with all the things he saw and probably did. I know he's struggling to keep it together—I see it every time he comes here. I think the dogs are helping. He seems at peace with 'em. Mentioned he had a lot of strays hanging around growing up. Told me how he joined up to get away from his Pa but not much more than that. Had a hard life no doubt.

He felt guilty about reading the entries. He needed to chew on them for a while to reconcile the straight-backed, high and tight form of his father with these words. The old man seemed to have a greater breadth of emotions than Cahill thought, or he'd begun to soften in his old age. It was a bit much to process after so many years, and for just a moment, Cahill wished he had some whiskey.

Inside his father's desk was a box of pictures. He flipped through a few on the top. They were mostly of the dogs. On the back of one that showed a Malamute-wolf with one blue eye and one brown was scribbled "Yona." He didn't recognize that one. He felt a stab of jealousy thinking his father cared more about all these damn dogs than he had about his own son. But then he dismissed the feeling as quickly as it came, telling himself, *Grow up, Dipstick.*

In the creaky guest bed that first night back home —he just couldn't sleep in his father's bed—Cahill lay on his back with his hands under his head, unable to sleep, listening to Mexican free-tailed bats and their babies sounding like nightingales. Sometimes he would hear them when his father woke him at five a.m., the bats' trills urging him outside, making it easier to rouse and wipe the crusty sleep from his eyes. He and Ardy would go for runs together in the still semi-dark, quiet except for the steady clink of his father's always-worn dog tags, the stars pulsing above and slowly weakening to nothing in the lightened sky by the time they made it back home. These were times that he had liked, perhaps even loved, his father.

Cahill grew accustomed to the veterans stopping by for weekly sessions and helping him with the dogs. A couple of times, he poked around to get information about Ardy, but the vets were pretty tight-lipped about his old man. He figured word had gotten around that he was missing and he took their reservation as a sign of respect. People in the country don't bring up family troubles or troubling family members. If Uncle Cooter goes crazy and burns down the family grocery store then ends up in the state facility, the story his family might tell is that it was a fluke electrical problem and Uncle Cooter is out of town visiting relatives. Saving face is next to godliness.

One morning a few weeks into Cahill's return, a vet named Lucius stayed after therapy to help clean the dog enclosures. He was a wisp of a man, but wiry, graying prematurely in his early thirties. He had a twitchy lip—explained it as a tic left over from a childhood neurological condition.

"Hey, you met ole' Hodge Madson yet? The one who was in Special Forces in 'Nam," Lucius asked while they scraped small pieces of chicken bone and meat off the ground before it became covered in flies.

Cahill remembered the name from his father's journal. "Nope, I don't think I have. He come around here a lot?"

"Yeah, he did. Far as I know he came twice a week for a good few years at least. Lives about forty minutes away in Dripping Springs, but he always made the drive." Lucius leaned an arm on his shovel.

"You don't say?" Cahill's curiosity was piqued, but he was also ready to be done with the dog chores for the morning. There was a bit of fence on the west side that needed tending and he wanted to get to it.

"I hear Hodge is getting pretty loony. Something about his meds and him having episodes. Luckily, or unluckily for him, he don't have no family." Lucius picked up the shovel and swung it onto his shoulders insouciantly, hanging his arms over like a lazy crucifixion. "We 'bout done here, boss?"

"Yeah, sure. Thanks for the help."

Cahill tended to the fence after Lucius left. He cut out a bad section with wire cutters and wondered what the deal with this Hodge guy was, why he'd been hearing the man's name so much, and if he'd ever show up to help with the dogs. And, the always-present question: where in the hell was his father?

*   *   *

The morning after the black creature shows up on the property, Cahill steps out the back door and sees that it's inside his yard near the double gates, its head still resting on its paws. Cahill looks to the gates and both are closed. *Goddamn thing must have torn a hole in the gate somehow.* But he can see from the porch that there's no hole.

The canine's citrine eyes follow him as he walks to the gate and bends down to take a look. It is less than five feet from him, but it doesn't move a muscle. *It had to have gotten out of the run somehow,* but there's nothing, no hole or any signs of gnawing. *That means the thing climbed ten feet straight up, then maneuvered over a two-foot overhang.* It was impossible. Cahill does not like impossibilities and speculations.

He addresses the animal. "What do you want? You don't eat anything and you eyeball me all day. Why don't you go about your rat chasing? Go on, git," he says, stamping his foot on the ground, but the dog stays where it is, looking indifferent. Cahill shakes his head, wondering why he let it in in the first place.

He has other things to do, though. The pack hasn't yet come in from the sanctuary and it's breakfast time. Their lateness makes him nervous. Resolving to keep an eye on the animal and also keep it away from the pack, he goes about his morning, hopping on the UTV that sits in the outbuilding to check the perimeter and see if he can spot the group of dogs. It's almost three miles around the property, all blackland prairie with Brushy Creek wiggling through the middle and a half-mile wide thicket of elm, burr oak, cottonwood, and hackberry huddled around it. East of the property, the creek meets up with the San Gabriel River and a tree and grass-filled savanna that surrounds it for miles.

The two-seater bumps over clumps of brown switchgrass, flushing out a covey of bobwhite quail that whistle their goodbyes as they fly scattershot. Rumbling by a persimmon Cahill's mother had planted for pies, he remembers the first time he cut one from the tree, not yet ripe. His mouth drew up, full of tannins, and he felt like he was chewing on aspirin and chalk, his tongue turning to fine sandpaper and rolling sideways out of his mouth like when you give a dog peanut butter, his cousins laughing at him. It took a while to get the taste out of his mouth. After that, he couldn't eat his mother's pies.

Cahill scans the fence as he goes, checking for issues, but finds his gaze wandering to the acres upon acres he can see for miles. Since coming back, he has been struck with how much of the surrounding prairie has gone under the plow: acres of corn, cotton, and hay where he and his cousins used to play in the tall grasses, running as far as they could through friendly neighbors' fields. There's no place for wild things on the prairie anymore, that much is clear to him.

On his return pass of the eastern fence, he sees the pack of eight wolfdogs snuffling near a tall stand of gamagrass. He whistles loud through his fingers and gets the attention of six, who bound toward him. He's worked with them every day, but a few still keep a respectable distance. Cahill knows they aren't afraid, just aloof, and probably have higher wolf content. He pets all the nearby dogs and looks each one over to make sure none are injured. When he's finished, he jumps on the UTV and whistles again so they'll follow back.

The six trot behind the vehicle as Cahill maneuvers along the last portion of fence toward the house. When he nears their enclosures, he notices a black shape sitting inside the sanctuary's fence. *It's that damn animal.* He floors the gas to reach it before a fight breaks out, but the dog just sits on its haunches looking his way. He stops quick in a puff of tire-strewn dirt and jumps out, the animal still sitting placidly near the gate, then looks to see where his dogs are. Every one of them has stayed far back, some moving in tight, nervous circles and others staring with their heads held low, lips rising over teeth in warning.

Cahill is relieved there will be no fight and opens the gate to the run. The black canine goes in without a problem. Warily, he moves past it and into the backyard, closing the main gate behind him.

He sits on a tree stump in the backyard, smokes, and thinks about what to do with it: let it out, poison it, shoot it, or . . . what?

Then a woman's clear voice yells, "Ardy, you home?" at the front gate.

Cahill crushes his smoke and ambles to the front. When he sees her he swears he hasn't seen a woman so feral looking in all his life. There are brambles and leaves in her tangled hair and the khaki pants and formerly white t-shirt that hang on her waifish form are all but shredded, as if she's been battling prickly pears. Her arms are thin but tight and he has a feeling that she's stronger than she looks, and perhaps a little older too. Her hips sling low on a long waist and when she speaks, she looks right at him. He's never seen eyes so green and dark, like a primeval, impenetrable forest. A scar runs from the corner of her right eye to the corner of her mouth. He wonders who could do that to such a face.

"Is Ardy around?" she asks, her demeanor self-assured as she sizes him up with her unfathomable eyes.

"No, sure isn't. He left a few months ago." Cahill doesn't know what to do with his hands, so he puts them in his pockets. This woman is dirty, but everything about her throbs with vitality and he is rendered self-conscious.

She looks at him sharply. "Left? Did you buy his property?"

He leans on the fence in what he hopes is a casual manner. "Not exactly. I'm his son, Cahill Womack. Nice to meet you." He pulls a hand out of a pocket and sticks it toward her. She's abashed but shakes it, her grip strong and warm.

"Sullie Fulton. It's been some time since I was around folks, been traveling. I seem to have lost my manners." She cracks a grin that is to him the first crocus peeking out of winter frost.

He asks her to stay for some sweet tea and ushers her to the porch.

When he returns outside with their tea in his mother's old Ball canning jars, she sips it politely, then sets it down on the old weathered spool that serves as a porch table. "Are you continuing the vet therapy, then? Your dad was a big help to a lot of people in the area."

"I am. There are a few that come out every week. Were you a part of the program?" He perches on his stool and imagines her in combat, figures she'd hold her own.

"No, but I did help your dad with the dogs. I've been working with them for years, traveling around to different sanctuaries. I used to stay in your Pa's guesthouse. I haven't been by in months and, frankly, I miss the dogs. Do you mind if I go back there?" She's expectant. This pleases Cahill.

He tells her yes, of course, so they head to the backyard.

"Woah, why's that one in the yard? He looks more wolf than dog."

Sullie bends down and puts her hand out for the black canine. It comes right over and, without sniffing, puts its head under her hand. She runs her fingertips over its topcoat, then yanks her hand back as if it has bitten her.

"You okay? Did it hurt you?" Cahill squares his stance, preparing to battle the damn animal, if need be.

An unreadable look on her face, she stands up and wipes her hands on her khakis as if to clean some gunk, subconsciously taking a few steps back while the dog stares up at her. "No, no, I'm fine. I, uh, thanks so much for the conversation and tea. I need to be heading out now since it's almost dusk. Got to find shelter before it gets real cold. I appreciate your hospitality."

Cahill is surprised by the abrupt conclusion to their meeting. He knows he wants her to stay, but he also knows her kind, had her pegged within a minute of meeting—she's stubborn and will balk if he's forceful. Something about her makes him feel almost desperate to be near her, which he's not at all used to.

"Well, you can always stay in the guest house again. Have a hot shower, some supper, and a full night's sleep in a proper bed. I'd hate for you to catch cold out there," he says, as light and noncommittal as possible.

She regards him for a moment, then turns her gaze to the animal. Cahill swears something passes between them. "I'll take you up on that," she says. "Thank you. In the morning I'll help out as repayment."

Sullie stays on and tends to the dogs. The black one becomes more skittish and paces outside the guesthouse at night, waiting for Sullie to emerge in the morning. During the day, it watches her try to lure the others to their enclosures with halved chickens and large chunks of bone-in beef. They whine for her from several hundred feet away and she gives up and goes to them with their dishes. After, they play and run through the fields.

"They don't like the black dog, Cahill," she tells him as they sit in the sunroom, the cold winter sun sinking past the trees clustered around the creek like people around a fire.

"Yeah, I know. I've been thinking about getting rid of it." He thinks that might sound harsh, so he adds, "But I don't want to hurt it, of course."

She side-eyes him from the faded green upholstered chair, worn threadbare to the batting on the arms. "That's good. He doesn't mean any harm. In fact, I don't think I've seen him eat or drink, so he might be sick."

He nods. "I guess we'll see. I've got veterans coming by in a few days, so I'll get their opinion. Maybe he can be of use to them." He isn't convinced, but he feels that Sullie has taken a shine to the creature. And he has taken a shine to Sullie, so he figures he better watch his step.

"I hope so. Oh hey, by chance are any of them Hodge Madson?" She picks at a hangnail.

Cahill looks at her. "That's the second time his name's been mentioned. Why the interest?"

"That would not surprise me at all. Honestly, he's a bit of a headcase. I tried to tell your Pa, but he took a liking to the guy. Said they had a lot in common and he really wanted to help him.

I don't know much about the guy, but he gave me the hibbity jibbities." She involuntarily shivers.

Cahill can't think of much to say to that. He halfway hopes Madson shows up so he can see what the fuss is, evaluate him based off what Sullie has said. Maybe he'd get some answers then.

At the end of Sullie's first week, Cahill studies her through the sunroom window while he enjoys his morning coffee. In the field beyond the pens, spidery panicles of bluestem and switchgrass spread on webbed mist and fog. A red-tailed hawk screams and glides low. Sullie slides between the pens and Cahill can already tell her mood by the slope of her shoulders. He likes the way she moves. Quick and low, with a subtle grace like a woman who knows what to do and what she wants. She keeps her sun-streaked, pecan-colored hair pulled back and stray locks fall into her face. She swipes them behind her ears. Cahill already knows that he's falling in love with Sullie, for her vigor and boldness as much as her beauty. She is quick to spark, like a live wire. He hasn't asked about her past, is instead patient. They banter each day and Sullie teaches him more about the creatures he came home for.

Later when they're out with the dogs in the field she says, "You know, most people think these animals are hybrids," and ruffles Nicodemus's chest fur. "But dogs and wolves have the same DNA, so they can breed with impunity. People can't take the wild out of them, no matter how much we breed them." Then she pulls on the dog's tail and runs, him bounding after her, her smiling, hair coming out of her ponytail and tossing wild behind her.

Cahill cooks her dinner that night. A roasted prime rib he found in the deep freezer, with seared carrots, potatoes, and cider from the cellar. They talk more about their respective lives and past loves, then the talk drifts to his father and mother.

"Were they happy when you were growing up?"

"I don't rightly know. I mean, I guess they seemed happy. But they also struggled with money a lot. Hard to say, really. My father's such a hard-ass all the time I could never tell what he was really feeling. But I'm sure you got that, having worked here with him." He waits for her response. Somewhere inside himself, though he can't recognize it as such, he yearns to learn more about the man he never really knew.

"He was real easy-going, actually. Never seemed to get flustered." She drinks some cider then clears her throat. "You know, maybe he changed. Twenty-five years is a long time."

"Yeah, maybe so."

She approaches him in the kitchen later when he's refilling their glasses. She comes in closer to him than she has since they met, looks right in his eyes and leans in past his mouth, taking a long sniff of his neck before bringing her lips around to his. Cahill pins her against the fridge and kisses her mouth, neck, shoulders. She unzips his pants and they fall upon each other with force, rutting on the kitchen floor until he thinks his lungs might burst.

After their sweat-slicked bodies cool next to each other, she sits up, slips on her shirt with an "I'm gonna go shower," and slinks toward the back door without looking back.

The next morning, Cahill's fixing breakfast and whistling "Hey, Good Lookin'" when Sullie comes in the back door and up behind him.

"I think I might head out," she says, looking through the kitchen window to the front gate and caliche road beyond.

Cahill's skin flushes and his stomach pitches, as if he's on a boat just trying to keep his feet under him. He pulls himself together before speaking. "I had hopes you'd stay on, Sullie. You're a big help with these dogs. Way better than me."

She puts her hands together on the countertop and stares out the window. "Look, things always go bad when I have . . . relations with a man." She turns to him, her verdant eyes shining with tears, and he sees the scar again and thinks about what horrors she can't yet express.

In front of him is an arresting creature who possessed him with a feeling he has not felt in many years. "We're fine. I'm like a rock, not going anywhere. Whatever you want to be, I'm game. I just enjoy being around you."

Sullie studies him for a few moments, seems to decide something, then simply says, "OK."

That afternoon, the black dog runs at Sullie and jumps, its paws aimed at her chest, and knocks her to the ground. Cahill grabs the damn thing to pull it off her, but she yells, "No!" with such a transfixed look that he abruptly stops, completely rattled. She sits up, maintaining contact with the canine. All afternoon and evening, she's catatonic by it, her fingers splayed on the umbral fur. When the moon crests above the creek's trees, she calls for a notepad and scribbles furiously for a long time.

They sit on his porch and drink sweet tea after she showers and eats ravenously of the beef stew he's made. Above them the stars are pinpricks in the dark lid of night.

"I've seen amazing things. Memories. You were in them. I don't even know where to begin." She flips through the notepad.

"What? My memories?"

"No, not yours. I don't know how to explain. Read this." And she thrusts the notepad his way.

I'm watching my son riding a blue Huffy bike through a field. His front tire catches a hole in the soil and he's flipped over the handlebars. I stride to him and he's crying, "Daddy, Daddy," and holding his knee. I'm pissed at myself, but I bawl him out. I pick him up and bring him inside . . . I'm jogging with my teenage son and trying to form my thoughts, to tell him things he needs to know about the world, about people, but it's hard for me. I'm not a talker. So we run together before dawn, morning after morning as he grows taller and taller and I say nothing . . . I'm taking care of my dogs and thinking about my son, who I haven't spoken to in years. What I would give to see his face again and tell him all the things I never could . . .

Cahill stops reading and looks up, setting his lips in a line. "What is this?"

"Those are the things I saw when I touched the dog." She folds her arms, as if she's already preparing for an argument.

"I think my father told you these things. Though the last one sure don't sound like him." He snorts.

"So you *are* the boy. Holy hell." Sullie takes a large swig of tea, finishing it off. "I'm gonna try that again." When she gets up to go, Cahill grabs her arm. She jerks it out of his grip and flashes him a look like she might murder him.

Moving his head back, just in case she lashes out, he says, "I'm sorry. I just don't want you to get hurt. I was real nervous today, watching you hunched by that thing. I don't think it's natural. Be careful?"

Her face softens. "I've worked with wolfdogs for years. I'll be OK," and smiles over her shoulder as she rounds the corner to the backyard.

She's sweating when she wakes and calls for him. He busts through the guesthouse door and she speaks as if she's in a trance: "We all trained at Fort Campbell together. Harris and I were buddies. They made me an E5 by the time we got to Vietnam, eight men under me, including Harris. I promised I wouldn't let them down, that I'd be a real leader. We were in Cu Chi, South Vietnam, with two battalions. Search and Destroy. We came into contact with the enemy at 1300 that day. We laid down suppressing fire and the platoon leader called us squad leaders back for briefing. When I returned, I found my men all bunched up. I was on their asses for not staying dispersed when an RPG screamed in and blew up, killing Harris and wounding myself and three others. I got myself up and yelled for Harris, but there were just pieces. Pieces everywhere." Sullie's crying and falls back on the bed. Her face goes immediately slack and she's fast asleep again.

Cahill takes his place outside the guesthouse window, thumbs out a Marlboro, clearly shaken up. He inhales and thinks about what all she said, some of it reminding him of stories his father told. He knew Ardy had been in Cu Chi, because he was in a field hospital there for what he'd said was just a minor injury. Cahill smokes half a pack and watches Sullie's supine form as the day darkens, then night deepens. Around two a.m., he wakes up with a start, his bent-back neck yelling at him. She's still in the same position, so he stumbles to bed.

Sometime past three a.m., she wakes him by flipping on his bedroom light. He squints at her pale, gaunt body, her wide-eyed, lined face.

"My dreams tonight. There's a path, through the trees, near the river. We have to follow it."

"What the hell?" Cahill one-eyes his alarm clock. "Do you know what time it is? It was just a dream, Sullie."

She seizes his hand and hers is feverish and thin. She says, "He loves you so much, Cahill. I feel like he wants you to know that, if nothing else." Her expression is ethereal, yet grave, the face of an exquisite madwoman. The face of the woman he realizes right in that moment he loves. So he gets up and dresses.

The scorched, sepulchral pines press in, stifling. It is very dark. Cahill's right arm wraps under Sullie's shoulder, supporting her. He muscles a path through the trees, breaking off small branches and pulling aside winter-browned whip vines with shiv-sharp thorns. Sullie points the old metal flashlight ahead of them as best she can, light slicing the mist in zig-zags when she stumbles, which is often. The black animal winds in front of them, under desiccated branches, between bare, black sticks that stab through the strata of dead leaves. Several times, Cahill thinks he sees the dog disappear, but it reappears a few steps later.

They come upon the cabin quickly, the flashlight's slight beam flickering as they stumble into the small cleared yard. It's as if it just appears in a space in the skeletal trees.

"There," Sullie says.

Cahill's heart thuds in his chest. The cabin is no larger than a child's bedroom and is in disrepair like an old forgotten shed. Its roof is made of dented and hole-rusted metal, with sheets of green plastic tacked on, and its sides are logs with scavenged pieces of flat wood nailed perpendicular and haphazard. There is one grimy, skewed window in the front.

The black dog pauses in the yard in front of them, then turns and waits.

Sullie stops and weakly says, "You go on. Help me onto the ground first." He helps her sit down on the gray powder where she slumps, ghostlike with lassitude. She looks up at him. The lines around her eyes are carved, the eyes themselves sunken and shadowed underneath. There is no longer a smile playing around her lips. "Go on. You've got to."

He paces toward the cabin and the dark dog. With each step, it's as if he's descending into a deep hole from which he knows he may never escape. As he approaches the flashlight reflects its own light in the dirty window like a feeble sun.

The animal reaches the small rough-plank porch. One moment

the dog is standing in front of the closed door and the next, it has gone through.

Cahill thinks he's imagined it and peers around the yard. He sees nothing and quickly strides the last steps to the window.

Stooping to peer in, he focuses the light past the accumulated dust and detritus, dead wasps and curled spiders. It flickers and goes out. He hits it a few times on his palm with a frustrated, "Dammit to hell," but it won't come back on.

Cahill peers in again, the crepuscular light only allowing him to see subtle shadows of movement by a ladderback chair, something furred and black, which can't be the dog, he reminds himself, because the door is still closed. He struggles with the logic.

The moving tenebrous thing curls around the legs of something on the chair, and then Cahill can no longer distinguish it from what is on the chair. He sweeps a sweaty knuckle across one eyelid, then the other, and looks again.

Someone is strapped in it, head bent back.

Cahill feels light-headed. The figure wears overalls like those his father used to wear. And there is a glint of silver hanging from the neck. After rubbing the glass with his sleeve and squinting, he still can't tell if it's a person or a scarecrow.

Does he have it in him to open the door and find out?

Cahill doesn't know anymore. He admits to himself that he doesn't much know anything like he thought he did.

He looks about wildly and focuses on Sullie behind him, now straining to lift her head off the ground, her own face ashen, drawn with worry and unmitigated sorrow.

Something inside him rips open like an old, unhealable wound.

He opens his mouth and wails.

For all the damn water in his eyes right then, all the years come and gone, the questions still unanswered and unknowable, he is a boy again, howling for his daddy. And that boy cannot bear to see, refuses to discern what is right in front of him through the Stygian glass.

The Continuing Controversy of The Snuggle Shack

Joe Dornich

Lonnie calls and tells me my first session isn't until noon, which is great because it means the protestors will be on their lunch break and not there to remind me that I'm a hell-bound gigolo. And a murderer. Of course, when I get to work there is a woman who has apparently brown-bagged it. She is perched on the curb with her protest sign across her lap, slowly destroying what appears to be an egg salad sandwich. She must spot my Snuggle Shack employee t-shirt, which advertises me as a "Certified Cuddler," because she bolts to attention, holding her sign high and proud. In bold, red letters, it reads: SNUGGLE SLUTS GO HOME! I want to ask this woman if she really thinks this is where I want to be. If she truly believes this is the life I always imagined for myself. But I don't. I just smile weakly and compliment her use of alliteration.

Across the street I see a giant hulk of a man, like an armoire with limbs. He's balding on the sides, and all the way bald up top, and the midday sun glints off of his huge, smooth dome. At first I think he's just another protestor, but he isn't holding a sign, or telling me what a terrible person I am. He just stares. He stares right at me. Then, the woman beside me starts screaming something about how I'm unraveling the fabric of this great and noble country, but it's hard to make out because her mouth is full of egg salad. I ignore them both and go inside.

Upstairs I find Lonnie in his office meditating beneath his eight watercolors of the Dalai Lama, and the photo of himself and Stanley Geegland. Stanley is Lonnie's friend from rehab who bares an uncanny resemblance to Bono. He even wears the little rose-colored glasses. Mindy and Allison, our two female snugglers, are in awe of the photo, and while Lonnie never outright says it's Bono, he doesn't correct them either. If Lonnie is aware of my presence, he doesn't acknowledge it. I knock on the doorjamb, interrupting what I'm sure is his inevitable Transcendence Into Enlightenment. Lonnie opens his eyes. He asks if my time away was mentally and spiritually recuperative. He asks if I am prepared to continue doing the healing work of Touch Therapy.

I say sure to both.

"I certainly hope so," Lonnie says. "The file is on the desk." Then he closes his eyes and continues his pursuit of Zen.

My first client of the day is one Sara Mews. According to her Snuggle Scenario we'll spend an hour in the Etruscan Room, on the bed, but above the covers. She has opted out of the Ambient Aural Therapy, which is great because that includes the Maui Waterfalls Fountain. That thing always makes me have to pee. Her file tells me that Sara suffers from social anxiety and mild depression. Her intake photo shows a thin, middle-aged woman who looks like she's never smiled in her life. I've seen mug shots with more glee. Even so, she's my first client since the incident, and I can't afford another suspension. Under her Preferred Therapy Postures, Sara has said that she'd like to start as the Little Spoon, but is open to some possible Face-to-Face. So that's how we begin.

Though Lonnie officially runs The Snuggle Shack, his dad is bank-rolling it. Mr. Johnson made his fortune inventing that white, foam tray beef is sold on. I guess before then meat was just wrapped in butcher paper, and the blood and other juices would leak out. Johnson's Meat Trays absorb those carnivorous reminders, and now they're in every deli and supermarket in the country. Mindy, Allison and I call him the Meat Diaper Man, though never in front of Lonnie.

The story is that a few years ago Lonnie was living with a vet tech, and at some point became addicted to canine oxycodone. He did a few failed stints in rehab, but the last one had more of a holistic, mind-body type of intervention. Lots of Touch Therapy and elephant gods. Whatever it was, it worked, and Lonnie's been gulping the Energy Exchange Kool-Aid ever since. He promised dad he'd stay clean if, in return, he'd help turn his new interests into a business. Lonnie used the money to convert the offices of a defunct law firm into three Snuggle Suites, each with a couch, pillow-top bed, adjustable lighting, and those ambient nature CDs. Though we've only been open a few months, and some people are coming around to the idea of Contact Medicine, most of the town thinks we're running some kind of new-age brothel.

My session with Sara does not go well. During Big/Little Spoon my arm keeps falling asleep, and strands of her hair drift into my mouth. I sneeze an unacceptable number of times. Though she remains stoically silent, I can tell Sara would be more relaxed if she were being buried alive. I suggest we try some Face-to-Face. This is a mistake. Snuggle Protocol requires that Face-to-Face include prolonged periods of therapeutic stroking along the shoulders and back area. Normally this is fine, but Sara has a number of pronounced moles on her back, like God, or Jesus, or whoever, superglued a handful of Raisinets back there before forcing her into this world. Every time I begin one of my stroking maneuvers, I run up against one of Sara's moles and stop short. I'm afraid of accidently lopping one off. Instead, I resort to a series of tentative, gentle pats that probably have little therapeutic value. It's like frisking a baby. Sara's disappointment is profound. Her mouth curls down, deepening already prominent frown lines. Her eyes stare at me with the lidless disinterest of a reptile. It doesn't help that our faces are about six inches apart. My Snuggle Summary Evaluation does not look promising.

It doesn't take long. I'm sanitizing the slippers with disinfectant spray when Allison tells me Lonnie wants to see me in his office.

He's still in the lotus position when I arrive.

"Take a seat please," he says.

There are no chairs in Lonnie's office, just a bunch of meditation pillows and a few yoga mats. I move to sit on a purple and gold cushion, but Lonnie says no. He means I should sit on the floor. So that's where I sit.

"I, we, all of us here are in the business of healing," he says. "And while of course the healing is our main objective, we depend on the business component to provide this service. The lights don't run on love, do they? I can't pay the rent on this place with smiles, can I?"

I admit that he cannot.

"So, until we all live in some kind of utopia where love and smiles are the primary means of commerce, we need the business. And that means clients. But you, you are driving those clients away from here, and in one case, right out of existence. At least, on this plane anyway."

Lonnie's talking about the woman I killed. Mrs. Dorothy Simone. Technically, she died of "natural causes," but that's a detail a number of people seem to be ignoring. Like the protestors. Like Lonnie.

"Each of us," he continues, "is striving for spiritual completeness. To find that harmonious balance between ourselves and our surroundings. We do this even though we know the journey will never end. Even though we know we will never be completely whole. Perhaps I've overestimated your position on this journey. Maybe, given your current level of wholeness, being a healing influence on others is asking too much. Does this make sense?"

I nod. I nod and try to ignore the fact that I'm having my "wholeness" judged by a guy who was once addicted to doggie smack.

"However," Lonnie says, "despite the unfortunate scene with Mrs. Simone, she did like you. As do the rest of our advanced clientele."

He means old people.

"So, until further notice, they will make up your client list. I will handle everyone else, as well as any walk-ins. Mindy and Allison, per usual, will take care of our male clientele."

"And when I'm not embracing the elderly," I say, "then what? What about the rest of my shift?"

"Equally divided between Maintenance and Housekeeping."

"C'mon Lonnie, you know I can't afford to change sheets all day. I need the tips."

"Then allow me to give you the most valuable tip of all," he says. "Unburden yourself from this negativity that is blocking your spiritual growth. Develop a calming, peaceful center, and allow it to expand and radiate out to others. Because, if you can't, you'll never know true serenity. Plus, I'll fire you."

Then Lonnie dismisses me, but not before giving me a copy of my written warning, which highlights the changes to my shifts. Lonnie's signed the bottom, and I notice he's dotted the "i" with a tiny yin and yang symbol.

A little piece inside of me dies.

I go back to work.

Mrs. Dorothy Simone was my regular nine-thirty Thursdays. She was a sweet old lady, though a bit eccentric. Always showed up for our session with her face completely made-up, wearing full jewelry and some sequined ball gown like she was off to celebrate the repeal of Prohibition. I'd remind Mrs. Simone that we couldn't snuggle with her dressed like that, and she'd bring a manicured hand to an overly rouged cheek, and feign embarrassment. *You know*, she'd say, *if you want me to slip into something more comfortable, all you have to do is ask.* Then she'd call me *troublesome*. Then I'd give her a pair of the pajamas we keep on hand for the lawyers and businesspeople who come in on their lunch breaks and don't want to wrinkle their suits.

We went through this routine every Thursday.

The day it happened, Mrs. Simone and I were snuggling on the couch in the Stillwater Room as usual, and after some time she put her head in my lap and I ran a brush through her sparse, pewter-colored hair. She fell asleep, leaving a drool stain on my pants that looked like an upside down South America. I didn't mind. When our session ended, I tried to gently shake Mrs. Simone awake. Then I used a little more force. Still, I got no response. Of course Lonnie freaked, though, to me, slipping away in a painless, peaceful slumber seems like the utmost degree of relaxation, and something of a testament to my abilities as a snuggler. Few saw it that way. Mindy wrote "The Cuddling Kevorkian" on my locker in red lipstick. Lonnie had to call for a Shutdown, and bribe the EMTs to take Mrs. Simone's body out the back. Even so, the protestors got wind of it, and now they have a whole other reason to hate us. We all got sent home early, which meant lost revenue, and more than a few unpleasant looks in my direction. Did anyone ask if I was okay? If I suffered any residual trauma from having a woman die in my lap? They did not. Was I praised for not mentioning the fact I wouldn't be receiving my usual twenty percent tip? I was not. What I did get was three days Reflective Suspension. I thought about quitting. Then I thought about the shameful six months of trying to shop around my degree in Television History, and the realization that I am unqualified for just about every job out there.

I'm in Laundry, trying to wrestle the duvets back into the duvet covers, when Lonnie sticks his head in and says phone. It's Gloria, the live-in I hired for Gramps. She says we have a problem. She says I need to come home right away. In the background I hear Gramps screaming that he's going to be late. Something made of glass breaks. I tell Gloria I'll be right there.

"I have an emergency at home," I say to Lonnie, "but I'll be back as soon as I can." He reminds me to breathe and focus on my bliss.

Outside, the protestors have returned from lunch en masse. When they spot me, their faces screw up in identical grimaces of judgment. They shout, and shake their signs—DOWN WITH COMPANION$HIP, A-LONE IS BETTER THAN A-JOHN— in my face, as if hoping to fling their righteous wisdom on me.

Across the street is the balding armoire man from earlier. His body goes rigid when he sees me, and his face mottles like ground beef. He moves to cross the street, ignoring or oblivious to the cars that have to stop short to keep from slamming into him. Just as he's about to reach me, a man steps between us. He says that I, and the work I do, are affronts to the Lord. His tongue darts in and out of his mouth when he speaks, and flecks of spittle land on my shirt. He holds a sign with a Bible verse written on it, and though I don't know it specifically, I imagine it refers to my way-ward soul, and the eternal hell-fires that will eventually consume it. Or something like that. The man says that I need to atone for my sinful ways, and accept Christ into my life, just as he has. Then he bops me on the head with the cardboard end of his sign.

I rush home.

When I arrive, I find Gloria chasing Gramps around the loveseat. Gramps is wearing his navy-blue pinstripe. Gloria looks more flustered than usual.

"I'm going to be late," Gramps says when he sees me. "This… woman here is making me very late."

On the floor, shattered into a dozen pieces, is one of mom's

Adorable Occasions figurines. It is—was—a calf and a tiger cub on a teeter-totter. I never liked that one. It never made sense to me, biologically speaking. Sure, maybe their friendship works for awhile, because they're young and don't know any better. But once that tiger cub grows up and realizes where he fits in this world, and what's expected of him, he's going to pounce off that teeter-totter and turn that calf into veal and wallets.

"What are you going to be late for?" I ask Gramps.

"Work of course. I have to be at the office by nine."

"No," I say. "You don't. You don't have to work anymore. You're retired."

Gramps looks around the room, and then at Gloria and me as if we've invaded his dreams. "I am?" he says.

"Yeah," I say. I take Gramps by the arm and lead him to his bedroom. His hands are trembling, and I help him remove his suit jacket and loosen his tie. It's amazing. Most of the time the poor guy has no idea where he is, or what's going on, but he can still tie the cleanest half-Windsor I've ever seen. It's like he's here just long enough to realize how fast he's going.

"This is not working," Gloria says as she sweeps up porcelain animal pieces.

"I know," I say, "and I'm sorry. I know he's been challenging lately, but there's a new medication, and maybe . . . "

"No, not just the Señor," Gloria says. "You and I. I have not been paid in three weeks. I cannot afford."

"Please. Just give me a few more days. Here," I say as I pull out my wallet, immediately and painfully aware of the futility of this gesture. I open it, hoping I guess that the pair of dollar bills inside have mated and reproduced. No such luck.

"Take this," I tell her. "I'll have some more for you soon."

But Gloria just stares at my meager offering and smiles. She spends more on the bus coming out here.

"I'm sorry," she says. "I cannot." Then she hands me the broom, grabs her purse, and walks out.

I stand at the window, hoping Gloria will change her mind, or at least glance back at us one more time. She does neither. Gloria becomes, along with Sara Mews, the second woman today to walk out on me filled with disappointment.

I'm on a roll.

I microwave some hotdogs for dinner, and Gramps and I settle in to watch his favorite show, *Pre-K MMA*. We're just in time for the main event. The announcer says today's bout features the toughest tots this side of the Mississippi: "Tiger" Timmy Witherspoon versus Preston "The Blade" Dempsey. The Tiger looks big for his age. Gramps suspects him of doping. The fight is less mixed martial arts, and more of an arms flailing, windmill type of exchange. The Blade has some good moves, but his head is too big for his body, and it keeps throwing him off balance. A couple of times the Tiger wanders off in the wrong direction and the ref has to reset.

"Your mother came to visit me last night," Gramps says in between bites of hotdog.

This is an impressive bit of news as mom's been dead almost a year now.

"Really," I say. "How's she look?"

"She's worried about you. She thinks you spend too much time alone. She wants you to meet a nice girl."

"Well," I say, "if you two somehow talk again, tell her I'm fine. Tell her I'm not lonely. I meet nice girls every day."

We watch the rest of the fight. In the third round The Blade trips on his own feet and bites his tongue. He cries on the mat until the ref counts him down, and the Tiger wins by technical knockout, and that's that.

I'm back at work on Tuesday, which is when the van arrives from Renaissance Gardens. The RG is a top-tier assisted living facility. I'd love to move Gramps there, but that place takes some serious bucks. I can't even afford the warped linoleum and wet bacon smells of Wavering Meadows. The protestors are pretty well behaved on Tuesdays, as most people are usually reluctant to yell at the elderly. Sure, some people still shake their signs, and chant how "Hugs Beget Whoredom," but most find it tough to sling their condemnation at someone's Bubby while she hobbles past in her pink housecoat.

I've brought Gramps to The Shack with me. It seemed like the best way to keep him out of trouble. Allison says she'll help keep an eye on him, and maybe work in a free Snuggle Session if there's time. Allison is great. She's my girl, or she would be if she only realized how much we had in common. Her dad left too, walking out on her, and her mother and brother when Allison was just a teenager. I guess her mother couldn't cope, because at the end of October that same year she hung herself from the oak tree in their front yard. Allison's little brother was the first to find her. He was too small to get her down, and none of the neighbors intervened because they thought she was an elaborate Halloween decoration. By the time Allison got home, her brother was sitting in the grass with his knees to his chest, rocking back and forth in the shadow of his mother. He's been in and out of the nut-hut ever since.

I want to take Allison out, maybe down to Cooler's Pub. We'd talk about our respective situations. How, because of her brother, and me with Gramps, we both know what it's like to sacrifice for a loved one. How we'd do anything for them, but sometimes, usually late at night, the thought of that responsibility sits like a weight on our chests, and it's hard to breathe. And even though helping them likely amounts to the one decent thing in our lives, it also fills us with a paralyzing sense of remorse, not to mention the crippling debt. Then, maybe after all of that, we'd share a plate of potato skins.

But I don't. I don't ask Allison out. I'm too shy I guess, or afraid she'll say no. Plus, I think she likes Lonnie.

The ladies from Renaissance Gardens keep me busy all morning. One client talks about her late husband, a tugboat captain, as she rests her head on my chest. She says her hands and fingers have become so thin she's had to move her wedding ring to her thumb, and since then nothing has felt the same. Another talks about how some of the women at the home cheat at Bridge. She insists on being the Big Spoon, and every time she recounts a lost hand, she gives me an angry little squeeze. Someone's grandma, who smells like buttered toast, spends the hour telling me about the time she was propositioned by Spiro Agnew in the elevator of a Baltimore Howard Johnson's.

Things slow down in the afternoon, and Lonnie decides I should use the free time to repaint one of the Snuggle Suites. Lonnie is always finding these weird paint colors that are supposed to have healing properties and evoke some kind of therapeutic something or other. The color he's picked for Suite 3 is called Shantung. Lonnie says it's the shade of the sun just as it rises. He says it's the

color of new possibilities, of seeing things in a fresh light. I say
it looks yellow to me, and Lonnie says that's exactly my problem.
Then he presses some money into my hand, and says four gallons
ought to cover it.

I decide to take Gramps with me. I find him in the Stillwater
Room, on the loveseat with Allison. His head is on her shoulder,
and she is holding one of his hands in both of hers. They've got
Rain on a Tin Roof playing as their Ambient Aural Therapy. I've
always liked that one.

Allison must hear me come in, because she looks up and smiles
at me. A strand of her chestnut-colored hair falls across her face.

Oh, Allison. When will our time come? When will we—free
from having to sweep up the little tumbleweeds of lint and hair
that collect under the beds, or having to constantly restock the
scented candles because they burn down so quick, because Lonnie
is too cheap to buy the good ones—have our moment? Some time
when we can talk, and not just idle chitchat, but about grander,
deeper topics. And maybe, during this conversation, one of us,
say me, makes a comment that, while on the surface is witty, also
speaks to a more profound, emotional understanding of things.
And perhaps, in response to this witty/emotional comment, one
of us, say you, laughs and gently touches my arm, letting your
hand linger for just a second. When will that happen?

Allison catches me staring at her, and her eyes seem to brighten,
as if lit from within.

Maybe now, I think. Maybe now is our moment. Then Gramps
catches me staring.

"Who the hell is this guy?" he asks.

Maybe not.

"Hi Gramps," I say. "You having a nice time?"

He turns to Allison. "Do you know this young man?" he asks.

Gramps always refers to me as a "young man" when he doesn't
recognize me.

"Sure," Allison says. "He's your grandson."

Gramps stares at her, and then me, giving us the same blank
look. Prerecorded rain continues to fall.

"I've got some errands to run," I say. "I think you should come
with me."

Gramps starts making this low, humming noise, and slowly

shaking his head.

"I'll take you to lunch," I say.

The humming stops and his posture straightens.

"Schotblatt's?" he asks.

That's just great. Gramps doesn't remember me, who he has known my entire life, but he can recall, with immediate clarity, the Reuben from Schotblatt's Deli.

"Sure. Schotblatt's it is," I say, and off we go.

As Gramps and I exit The Shack, the protestors quiet down, and step aside, creating a little path. I think, finally, I'm catching a break.

But no. The protestors aren't stepping aside for me. They're making room for the Bald Armoire. He stops a few feet in front of me. He's got a look of concentration on his face that makes the skin around his eyes crinkle.

"Was it you, or the other guy that done it?" he says.

"Done what?" I say.

"Killed my mama."

Growing up, mom always said that I had a smart mouth. That I didn't think before I spoke. She said that one day my smart mouth would get me in trouble.

And she was right. Because instead of apologizing, or explaining what really happened, or offering any measure of sympathy, I say this: "Holy crap! Mrs. Simone was your mom? I never knew she had a son. In all the time we spent together, she never once mentioned you."

I know, as the words leave my mouth, that this is probably an ill-advised response. The Armoire winces. Then he does this ragged-type breathing through his nose that makes his massive chest rise and fall. Then, as if to confirm my suspicions, he pulls a gun from the waistband of his jean shorts and shoots me.

The Bald Armoire shoots me right in the stomach. I can't believe it. The impact knocks my right on my rear, which, oddly, hurts more than the bullet and fresh hole in my gut.

The gunshot creates a panic. The protestors flee in every direction, their abandoned signs littering the sidewalk. Even The Armoire seems to have disappeared. The peace and quiet is a welcomed change, even if it, I suppose, comes at a hefty price.

I lie back and stare at the sky. There are no clouds.

After some time I feel my shoulders and head rise, and I think this is it, my body is ascending to that vast and mysterious beyond just like movies and TV always promised. Then I'm disappointed that even death has become a cliché. Then I feel the scratch of polyester against my cheek, and realize it's Gramps pulling me into his lap.

"There, there young man," he says as he gently pats me on the head. "Help will be along soon. Try to lie still."

And even though it hurts my neck, I tilt my head back to look at my grandfather. He looks down at me, and smiles, and continues to stroke my hair.

"You know," he says, "my grandson is taking me to lunch today."

I look away. I close my eyes.

You would think that after so many times of Gramps forgetting who I am, that it wouldn't hurt anymore. But it still does.

It hurts every time.

Rituals

Daniel Bullard-Bates

I met Katherine and Jared on my first day in Chicago. The graduate school helped me find an apartment close to campus. I met a few other students in passing as I carried boxes from the rental truck to my new front door. It was fall, and more than once when I stepped outside I paused to feel the cool breeze in my hair and admire the just-changing leaves.

With the last of the boxes moved, I stood in my bare-walled living room wondering how to start unpacking when Katherine, sweet, beautiful Katherine, my poor Katherine, who I loved, first knocked on my door.

Chestnut brown hair kissed her bare shoulders. Freckles wandered well beyond the borders of her cheeks. She wore a red silk dress and thin freshwater pearls. If she had reached out her hand I would have taken it. I didn't speak, having no idea how to welcome her into my life, and she smiled and invited me over for dinner.

"The department told my partner that you're in his program. We're having some friends over for dinner tonight and we'd love for you to join us."

I'm pretty sure I thanked her, asked her when it would start, and mumbled something about having to double-check my calendar.

I've never kept a calendar.

A trail of ants was winding its way through my bedroom, the refrigerator was empty, and I didn't even have a bed.

I was late to dinner, having spent too much time picking a tie and a bottle of wine. Katherine greeted me at the door. She looked surprised to see me but her smile was immediate and genuine, like I was already an old friend that she was hoping to see.

"We didn't think you could make it," she said. "Sorry. We started without you."

She thanked me for the wine and introduced me around the room, starting with Jared. He wore a t-shirt and jeans, and I clung desperately to his handshake while I noted with increasing panic that the other three guests were in similarly casual attire.

"Guess Katie makes for a sort of misleading invitation. Should have told him there's no dress code, hon." He nearly concealed a southern drawl.

"Well, I think the rest of you should take notes," Katherine said as she took her seat. She passed me a heavy wooden bowl full of salad and stage whispered, "None of these fuckers know how to dress."

"Try the rolls," said the guy to my right. "Jared's been cooking all day."

I can't remember his name. It doesn't matter. I'm not sure I ever saw him again. Their friends were nice enough. Mostly I kept quiet.

It wasn't until after dinner that the other guests finally left. I got up to leave with them, but Jared asked me if I wanted to hear one of his favorite bands and Katherine was rolling a joint so I sat back down.

Passing a joint is both intimate and ritualistic. Everyone's lips press against the same paper. We all pass to the left. A sharp inhale of breath and awkward pause.

In most social situations or anywhere out in public, we wear a harmless, polite personality like an extra skin. People aren't really like that. Good friends are the ones you can let past the skin. They're the ones you can relax with. Sometimes marijuana helps.

"It seems to me," Jared said, his words trailing smoke as he exhaled, "that there's a lot of evidence for alien life in the Bible."

Katie rolled her eyes. "Not this again."

Jared took another hit and passed it to me. "Mysterious, impossible, immortal beings, existing outside of our normal conception of reality, appearing only in visions and dreams. Does that sound like an angel or a telepathic alien to you? People keep wondering when we'll make first contact when divine inspiration has been part of human history for thousands of years."

"I mean, maybe you're right, but trying to explain religion is dangerous," I mused. "Or the world, for that matter. If you think you can explain it, you're probably just oversimplifying it."

Jared laughed. "The poor bastards on your thesis committee."

"I mean, maybe gods are just extraplanar aliens, maybe the mythologies are right, and maybe they're elaborate social constructions born of a culture-wide fear of death. Does it have to just be one way?"

"You two are super high," Katie said.

I was embarrassed, for a moment, worried I'd been rambling like a fool, but Jared just said "yup" and Katie started laughing and couldn't stop and then tried to take another hit and coughed and spluttered, and soon we were all laughing and I forgot to be afraid.

I told them my college mentor's story of the exorcism he performed in a tiny home in rural China, which reminded Jared of a paper he wrote for a class on magic, science, and religion that he took in Georgia, and Katie told us about a book she'd been reading about the arcane practices of the English pagans. I was swimming with ideas, sitting with the two brightest minds in the world, finally right where I wanted to be, finally wrestling with the very nature of faith and reality. This was everything I wanted from graduate school and I hadn't even entered a classroom.

"I wish I believed in magic," Jared said, lying on the floor. "When I was little, Grammy had me convinced that fairies lived in the backyard. I spent hours out there, just talking to them. Kind of embarrassing now that I think about it."

"Well, I think it's fucking adorable," said Katie, rolling another joint.

"Me too," I said, and we laughed again.

I was sprawled on the couch, too relaxed, bold and foolish. "I think you two are my soul mates." I was already saying it, not even considering what it must sound like. "I think this is what I was always meant to do. Thank God," I said, "or whatever powers, that I chose Chicago. This feels like destiny."

What an ignorant piece of shit I was then. If only I'd gone elsewhere, or better, stayed at my dead-end job. If only I were answering telephones and Googling dull topics for a boss who was never satisfied. (Hypothesis: It enthralls victims through their passions. It draws them in with the familiar, not the otherworldly.)

It's my fault. Two years ago I opened my mouth and set it all in motion.

I asked them if they'd ever tried any of it. They asked me what I meant and I said, "Magic. All those rituals and arcane traditions: spells, bindings, ceremonies of love and rain and wealth and sex and happiness. Not this new-age hippie shit, and take no offense, because I'm part hippie too." Jared chuckled and raised his glass as I pressed on. "I mean, we could try the real thing, trace the symbols and speak the mantras. Aren't you curious to know if it works?"

And of course we were curious. Aren't you?

Look at us: Katherine in her red dress lounging on the couch and lighting up, me in my collared shirt and loosened tie gesticulating wildly, Jared in his t-shirt and jeans lying on the ground. They're both looking at me and smiling. He looks the odd man out but I was the stranger. I imposed myself. I interrupted their lives.

I can't believe he's dead.

It was Katherine who came up with the plan.

"A spell is like a hypothesis: if you move this way and chant these words while offering these materials, then something incredible might happen. Rain or love or whatever it is you're looking for." She was pointing her leg straight up into the air as she reclined on the couch, the hem of her dress teasing us both as it slipped up her thigh, her smile coy and confusing when she caught me looking. "So we could work our way through the ritual tropes of modern and ancient civilizations, experiment with acts and ingredients, try different symbols and languages, and track the results."

She made it sound easy. Worse: she made it sound safe.

High-pitched barking, shattering glass, and a man and a woman yelling sounded from the apartment above. Katherine got up, smoothed her dress, and phoned the police. Neither of them looked surprised. It wasn't the first time.

"Shitty way to end a good night," Jared said. "But it's getting late. Swing by tomorrow. Let's keep talking about this."

That night I sat on the floor of my bedroom watching the highway of ants march through it. I crushed them, one by one, and muttered with each pressing of my thumb, "Next life, you kill me." It was useless. By the time the police pulled up outside, an hour or more after Katherine's call, all I had to show for my efforts was a pile of dead ants and a wider river of living ones. They just marched around the bodies.

I unrolled my sleeping bag in the living room and stared at the ceiling until I finally fell asleep.

The first week of classes passed without incident as Katherine, Jared, and I made plans. I did my classwork and bought ant traps. Mundane concerns.

Our first ritual was a simple cleansing. We burned sage, cedar, and sweetgrass in our apartments, pushing negative influences out of open doors and windows and filling the corners of each room with sweet-smelling smoke.

I spent more and more nights at their place. We made small talk over dinner, about our classes, our students, our histories. When dinner was done, we turned our attention to a new tome or grimoire: *John Dee's Five Books of Mystery* or the *Clavicula Salomonis*. We assigned ourselves readings by areas of interest and expertise— one week I read *Crowley's Liber ABA Book 4* while Jared studied Agrippa's *Three Books of Occult Philosophy*. Katherine researched anthropological accounts of witchcraft and sorcery in Southeast Asia.

Back then our study was a fledgling thing, no more than a pastime. At times it just felt like a book club. I didn't expect it to go anywhere.

It was Katherine who took the most detailed notes, filling her notebook with diagrams and symbols. She took to calling it her Book of Shadows, in jest at first, but it was her list that we consulted when it was time to gather supplies.

Jared took the L to a new-age store and came back with pouches of powder and symbols wrought in silver. Katie drove to a gem and mineral shop to pick out crystals. I went to Chinatown and found a little shop where I rifled through incense.

They gave me the cheapest task because I was the poorest. They didn't even mention it. Their generosity came naturally and they asked nothing in return.

We collected candles from our apartments, borrowed chalk from a classroom, and visited pawn shops looking for oddities.

With all our materials gathered, it was time to plan our first real undertaking.

That night, Jared made eggplant parmesan and Katherine poured a bottle of red. One of our most ancient rituals is the shared meal. The host offers protection and sustenance, the guest offers respect and gratitude. How many ancient and modern cultures have prohibitions against breaking this sacred bond?

As she poured me a second glass of wine, Katie said that we ought to summon some rain. It had been particularly dry for the last month, and the success or failure of our spell would be easy to measure. It would rain or it wouldn't.

In sympathetic magic, the part represents the whole. Objects retain their connections even at a great remove. A twig could be used to represent and affect the tree. A bit of stone would be needed to cast a spell on the mountain it came from. A drop of blood may have the power to control a human being. And so on.

Their apartment was our ritual space. We moved the couch and chairs and rolled up the rug to make room. A jug of water for the rain, a stone bowl for the earth. No chalk circles then. No fires. A quiet room, pouring water, a soft chant.

After half an hour we had nothing to show for it but a light breeze through the windows and a few clouds on the horizon. For all we knew they were there when we started. Katherine shrugged and started to clean up. Even though nothing had happened, the ritual act had been so calming and lovely that I felt at peace. I don't think any of us really expected it to work. A little disappointed, perhaps.

Hours later, when we were all reading in our separate corners, the room began to darken. Katherine walked to the window.

"You guys?"

Thick clouds covered the sky. We joined her, staring up. The air felt electric. I could feel a buzzing between us, and then a sense of relief as the first few drops of rain struck the ground. Within moments the streets were drenched.

"No way," Jared said.

Katherine ran outside to dance in the rain despite the autumn cold. Jared checked the forecast. I stood at the window watching Katherine spin on the grass outside, mouth wide open, her clothes already soaked. Jared told me there was a ninety-percent chance of thunderstorms that day. We were so busy studying how to call down rain that we hadn't even realized it was on the way.

And yet: we might still have caused it.

Magic is unpredictable, and its laws are not our laws. Our ritual may have reached back to form those clouds, may have blown them over Chicago, may have put everything into place.

It rained for hours.

We initiated ourselves. There are many secret societies devoted to magic and mystery, and their initiation rites are closely guarded, but for those with a longer history we found enough. We pieced together rituals from the Hermetic Order of the Golden Dawn, Thelema, the Rosicrucian Order, Ordo Templi Orientis, and other prominent western magical traditions. Where our primary sources failed us, we looked to histories and biographies, finding that Aleister Crowley had his hands in as many secret orders as he could find.

Our rituals that winter had no measurable results, nor were any expected. Instead we sought to open our third eyes to see and understand that which was beyond normal sight. We were expanding our powers, calling gods and spirits to witness and affirm our transformation from ordinary human beings into initiates or neophytes. Theoretically we would need someone of a higher order to grant us entry, but when we sought out the modern-day orders they seemed absurd. One website offered instant magical training for a registration fee. We figured we were better off on our own.

Our interest waxed and waned into spring and summer. Some days we would sit in focused meditation for hours. On others we would descend into giggling fits dressed in robes and hoods, anointing one another with oils or touching swords to shoulders. We practiced the pronunciation of languages living and dead, learning to speak with gravitas and confidence.

We formed our own order, learning to trust each other, rely on each other, turn to each other in times of need.

Near Halloween, Jared's grandmother was diagnosed with breast cancer and he rushed home to see her.

It was strange spending time with Katherine when Jared wasn't there. We watched scary movies and went to an all-night diner to talk when Katherine didn't think it was safe to sleep. We went for a long walk in the park and huddled together on a bench since we forgot our jackets. I put my arm around her.

She talked about Jared's grandma: how she and his mother raised him together, the pale yellow house they all lived in, next to corn fields in the middle of nowhere in Georgia. The pies she made. How thin the walls were in that house.

That Saturday night I kept asking her what she was thinking. I wanted her to be thinking about me as much as I was thinking about her. I wanted her to say something that would let me bring up how much I wanted her. She always had an answer but it was never the one I was looking for. We were sitting on the couch talking about Scientology. Some hair fell into her face and I moved it behind her ear. My fingers brushed her cheek. Her lips parted. I wondered whether I should kiss her. She laughed and turned away.

Jared came back the next day. Standing out on the sidewalk, he said his grandmother was starting chemo and the doctors didn't know whether it would work. He started to cry, and Katherine and I wrapped our arms around him and held him close. He gave us both a squeeze and said, "Hope y'all didn't prove magic is real without me." We assured him that we hadn't and walked inside together.

They seemed closer in those days, but I started to notice a tension between them. When we went out to parties they were overly cute with each other, but around me they let their guards down. Jared criticized Katherine's decision-making or word choice. She started drinking more. As fall turned to winter, the clean Chicago snows turned to piles of dirty brown slush that seemed like they would never melt.

We continued to experiment, but we frequently cancelled planned rituals to seek out some other source of fun. We rarely left the building. In the dark and the cold, we traveled between our homes and our classes like they were island sanctuaries in a sea of discomfort. We put off going outside until it was absolutely necessary.

The upstairs neighbors fought more and more. They still walked their dog but never far. The husband would take the dog around the block, yelling at it whenever it misbehaved and threatening to hit it when it pulled on the leash. It was almost a funny sight, the huge, red-faced man yelling at a shaggy, off-white poodle, but I felt sorry for the dog.

The wife wasn't exactly kind to it, but at least she let it be. She would just stand out on the sidewalk smoking a cigarette while the dog explored, bounding through filthy snow and staining it yellow.

I passed her once on my way into the building. She had a large, puffy coat with the hood up, but I could still see the bruise around her eye and on her round cheek. I asked her if she was all right and she said she was fine. There was nothing I could do.

Jared, Katherine, and I smoked a lot more pot that winter. Katherine, worried about our lungs, bought a vaporizer. On days when we didn't have classes we spent most of the day high, watching shows, playing video games, and talking. We stopped working on our rituals entirely for the month of December, and then Jared and Katherine went to Georgia for Christmas. Jared invited me, but I couldn't afford to go. My father offered to fly me home but I didn't want to. I spent the holiday alone and went out for Chinese food.

When they came back, Jared knocked on my door. He asked me to join them for dinner and said there was something they wanted to talk to me about. He didn't hug me and he avoided my eyes. My heart was in my throat when I asked if I could bring anything.

He looked at me and smiled. "Just yourself."

I let myself exhale.

When I came over, Jared answered the door. Katherine was already at the table, which had a table cloth on it, candles lit, and wine poured. I felt like I was intruding on a romantic evening. I hesitated in the doorway, but Katie beckoned me to sit down. She was wearing the same red dress she wore the night we met. I couldn't keep my eyes off her. Jared was finishing something in the kitchen and we sat mostly in silence, sipping our wine. Katherine told me that Jared's grandmother was feeling a little better and that she hadn't lost any of her considerable powers in the kitchen. It was too early to tell, but recovery still seemed possible.

We fell into familiar rhythms as we worked our way through a bottle of wine, a potato leek soup, and a mushroom risotto. Jared had really outdone himself. I'd forgotten that they wanted to talk to me about something by the time Katherine uncorked a second bottle and Jared took an apple pie out of the oven.

"So we've been talking," Katherine said, looking down at the table, "and we think we should consider adding another element to our research."

"Yeah?"

"If you're comfortable with the idea," Jared started, putting the pie on the table. Steam rose from it, filling the air with the smell of apples, sugar, and cinnamon. He looked at the pie as he continued, "we think we should explore, uh," he swallowed awkwardly, "god, I thought I knew how I wanted to say it."

"All right, now you're making me nervous," I said.

Katherine laughed. "Right, I'll just say it then. You totally have veto power on this, but we've agreed that we'd like to try our hands at carnal rites." She smiled, and looked at Jared again, who nodded and focused on cutting the pie. "I mean, if that makes you uncomfortable, you can just forget we ever mentioned it."

Jared served me a slice of pie and watched me for my response.

"What, uh, what would we . . . " I trailed off and took a large sip of wine.

Katherine spoke like she did in front of a classroom of under-grads. "There are a number of traditions that require sexual acts or the fresh products thereof. Jared and I would, you know, provide that. And you'd be there, doing whatever else was needed."

Did I notice or imagine her reluctance? I thought I detected disappointment in her voice. I didn't see the whole picture then.

I didn't know if I could handle it, watching them together. But they were beautiful and I was curious and drunk, so I took another swig and asked, "When do we start?"

Katherine smiled, finished her glass, and poured herself another. I couldn't tell if Jared was excited or terrified. I couldn't tell if I was excited or terrified. When Katie got up to go to the bathroom, I noticed a large bruise on the back of her shoulder. It looked like a bite mark, maybe several.

That Saturday night we drew a chalk circle, placed our totems, and lit candles. We passed a cup and drank from it. We spoke the words. Outside it was snowing.

Jared and Katherine stood as I called and they responded. We didn't need our books any more. We were learning the languages.

The phrasing was always simple and resonant. It stuck in your head once you understood it.

Katherine took off her t-shirt and Jared took off his. A Celtic cross on a shoestring hung against his chest. I had never noticed that before. Katherine glanced down at me but Jared's eyes were only on her. He took off the cross and set it on the floor outside the circle.

When it was over, I blew out the candles while Jared put his pants back on and Katherine walked to the bathroom naked. When she came back she slipped on her underwear and t-shirt and rolled a joint. None of us said anything, but we were all smiling.

Katherine laughed.

"What?" Jared asked.

"Nothing."

Katherine held up the joint and walked into the bedroom. We followed and lounged in their big bed, smoking with Katherine between us. Eventually we drifted off to sleep.

(Hypothesis: the mere act of magical performance weakens the boundaries of the world. It doesn't matter which rituals are attempted or whether they seem to fulfill their purpose; all that matters is sincerity. If true, are the results personal, local, or global? And what waits on the other side? What pushes against the soft outer membranes of our lives and minds?)

I woke up to Katherine kissing my cheek.

"Jared made French toast," she said. "He got Vermont maple syrup, just for you."

I wiped the sleep from my eyes and walked out to the table.

Jared was humming and smiled at me when I came in. "Almost ready. Want some orange juice?"

I was worried things would be strange, but they were fine. Better than fine.

It was Katherine who finally mentioned it, and when she did she said, "Well, I don't know about you two, but I think our experiment last night was a huge success."

Neither Jared nor I responded except by staring down at our breakfasts and smiling to ourselves.

We did the next ritual on Thursday. That was the first time we'd performed during the week, but it wouldn't be the last. After our third sex rite, that Saturday night, Katherine thought it seemed strange that I still had all my clothes on when they were so exposed. I recommended that we start the next ritual nude instead of disrobing. We were already experimenting with the ritual objects, languages, phrasings, and patterns.

"We should never be afraid to change something if it doesn't seem right," Katherine said. "Religion and intuition are deeply related. How else could religion have started?"

They didn't look at me often when they were together, but they did look. They must have noticed. It was impossible to hide.

It was my birthday. I'd mentioned it a few weeks before, but neither of them seemed to remember and we had plans to continue our experiments that night.

Jared welcomed me in, hiding something behind his back, and then they both shouted, "Surprise!" and rattled noisemakers and blew on cheap plastic kazoos.

There were paper birthday hats and Jared had a cake in the oven. There were olives and fresh-baked bread and sun-dried tomatoes and brie. There was chicken simmering in red wine on the stove and he was stuffing baked potatoes and putting them back in to bake again. Katherine smiled, wished me a happy birthday, and gestured me to my seat.

I asked if there was anything I could do to help and Jared said, "Not today!"

Katherine handed me a glass of wine, a joint, and a lighter.

The food was incredible, and just when I was too full to eat any more there was chocolate cake.

"How the fuck did I get so lucky?" I wondered and Jared clapped me on the back.

"You deserve the best," he said.

After dinner, Katherine went to check her e-mail and Jared and I dragged ourselves to the couch. I collapsed and he moved my legs so they were on his lap.

"So, I've got something I want to talk to you about," he started, then hesitated.

"Should probably talk to me about it, then."

"This is kind of awkward. Okay. Remember when we got back from Christmas?"

"Yeah."

"Well, before we left Katherine and I weren't getting along too great. I thought she was gonna leave me. Sometimes when I thought about her leaving me I thought she might leave me for you. I thought about the two of you together. I was pretty freaked out about it but after a while…" he trailed off as Katherine came back in and sat in the chair by the couch.

She smiled at him. "Don't let me interrupt."

Jared took a deep breath and looked down at the floor. I followed his eyes and saw the faint remainder of the chalk circle there.

"Well, I talked to her about it and she said she did like you but wasn't going to do anything about it. I felt, well, I felt kind of disappointed. I told her I liked thinking about the two of you together. And we, well, we had a really good night that night. First good night in a long time." Jared took a deep breath. "You two are just—you're such cute nerds together. You're shy with each other and it's so fucking adorable. Sometimes I feel like I'm watching a show with some kind of will-they-won't-they, and after thinking about it a lot I really hope you will. I think you'd make each other really happy. I think you'd give each other things that you need that you aren't getting anywhere else. And I think it sounds like it could be really hot."

"Wow," I said. "I mean, really? The idea doesn't freak you both out? I mean, yeah, I have a big crush on you, Katherine."

"Obviously," Jared said.

Katherine smiled and bit her lip. "We've been talking about it a lot. We both feel safe with you. And yeah, big-time crushing over here."

"Sounds like a yes to me!" Jared said, and did a few tiny, adorable claps. "I'm gonna go for a walk, y'all."

Katherine and I started slowly. Our first kisses were shy. We spent a few nights just cuddling before we tried to have sex, and the first time we did try I was so nervous that I didn't stay hard for long. I apologized and she petted my head and told me we had time. She thought it was cute. She asked me what I was worried about and I said that I just didn't want to mess things up between us.

The next time we tried I wasn't nervous anymore.

Jared and Katherine were happier in that time than I remember them ever being. They were sweet to each other and Jared and I grew even closer. We spent more and more nights cuddling in their big bed, trading out who got to be in the middle. We had a lot of talks about boundaries and how we should be around each other, and before long Katherine felt free to kiss us both when it was just the three of us. Jared and I exchanged curious looks from time to time, and I wondered if he wanted to kiss me. I wondered if I wanted to kiss him.

When we were around other people it stayed our secret, and there was something thrilling about that, too.

From the beginning we all knew we wanted to do another ritual with Katherine and me at the center, but it took about a month before we were all comfortable enough to try it. We'd been taking a break from the study, focusing on our classes and each other, and we didn't realize how much we had missed it until we started to clear the furniture. We were all giddy, excited. Maybe scared, but it didn't matter.

We got loud that night. Loud enough to wake the neighbors. When we were done, Katherine collapsed on top of me and Jared rubbed her neck. She sat up with me still inside her and kissed him. He looked down at me and asked if he could kiss me too. I nodded, begging silently for him to do it.

The next morning we woke to the sound of knocking on the door. Jared threw on some clothes, closed the bedroom door, and went to answer it. Katherine rolled over, pressed herself against me, and kissed me.

When we came out of the bedroom, the husband from upstairs glanced at us suspiciously. "All I know is I heard some weird shit," he said, looking around the room.

I saw how strange it must have seemed: the carved wooden figures buried in the dirt around a small pine tree, the crystals hung to refract the light, the herbs on the windowsill, the old books lying open to pages of arcane symbols.

"We'll try to keep it down." Jared's ease made it seem like we were all just having a laugh. "Really sorry about that."

Eventually he left.

"Where the fuck does he get off?" Katherine said. "We're not hurting anyone."

She would never hurt someone. It wasn't her fault, what happened. She didn't know. None of us knew. She couldn't have known.

Moving into spring, our experiments became more frequent. The rituals we performed were about lust, love, and life. Whether it was us or the rituals, something was working. I felt full and satisfied. There was nothing I wanted to change. I just wanted them and us and our studies and I had it all. I was experiencing a thing that already lends a supernatural feeling to ordinary life: passionate new love. I would have done anything to be with them. To stay with them.

Maybe I'll be with them again.

Once, I asked Jared if he was ever jealous.

"I was jealous for a while," he said. "But honestly, I was the most jealous before the two of you had even kissed. When you showed up she just gave you so much attention. You didn't talk much, but when you did she hung on your every word. She didn't look at me the way she looked at you. But now why would I be jealous? I have both of you. You're the world that matters. You're my every day. Maybe it's a little weird every once in a while, but it is so fucking worth it."

I kissed him then, for the second time. His lips were softer this time, more receptive.

Katherine walked in on us and said, "Damn."

We pulled away.

"Oh shit, don't stop," she said, giggling.

Jared always had this calm about him that I found soothing, like nothing a person said in his company could disturb or surprise him. He looked relaxed in any position, and would drape himself over furniture in ways that were no doubt terrible for his back but made him seem perfectly at ease. He didn't have a strong accent from his Georgia days, but the remnant of a lilt in his voice made me nostalgic for a home I'd never known.

I wanted to see him running through a corn field. I wanted to wrestle with him and his dogs on a hot day and be called home for dinner where I could watch him drink a tall glass of lemonade and hear him sigh. When he showed me pictures of himself as a child he was just as I'd imagined: tousled hair, an easy grin, smudges of dirt on his clothes.

We were all losing interest in school. We thought we were learning deeper truths. Not just about the rituals and traditions of the world, but about sex and love and ourselves, about new ways to build relationships. I was happy then.

Can you ever remember what it feels like to be happy once it's gone? I'm so tired now. I just feel numb.

We navigated by sensation and let emotion guide us. We planned less and less, only agreeing on the components beforehand and then seeking moments of bliss. We determined success by the pleasures of the body and the exultation of the mind. We recorded our results by the potency of our emotions. We started to favor certain herbs, symbols, and languages over others.

If I exorcise the details it is only to protect you. Don't look for the notes. Don't repeat the experiments. I'm still recording the results, and they are clear. There's something there. It shouldn't be. It shouldn't exist.

(Hypothesis: my mind may be beyond repair. It is impossible to know the extent of the damages. Its presence makes hope or clarity impossible.)

Why am I still here? Why wasn't I taken?

They asked me to move in that summer to save on rent so we could focus on our research. We shared everything. It was shortly after that when Jared and I became more intimate.

I deserve what's coming. They were happy before I met them, or if not happy, happy enough. Better to be unhappy than to live through this.

Can a love be too deep, too profound, too supportive?

We were good to each other, we were in love, and we let our support and our fascination carry over into the rituals. If we had only found each other, only discovered our connection, only fucked and loved and talked and comforted each other, only bared our hearts and bodies to each other, we might still be together. It was good, what we had. It was safe.

But we let our curiosity take us too far. One of us should have called an end to the rituals; someone should have drawn some boundaries on what we would try, on the forces we would seek to summon and control. None of us knew it could be dangerous. We were still skeptics. We hadn't experienced anything we couldn't explain.

There's something stuck in my teeth. I can't get it out. I can feel it with my tongue but I can't reach it with my nail.

We were all happy for a time, but I broke the spell. I brought death into the circle.

We were holding hands and speaking in a droning hum. I opened my eyes and watched a bead of sweat trickle down Jared's chest. The fan turned and the candles flickered. Cool air rushed around my naked body. Jared opened his eyes and smiled at me. A moth flew between us.

I didn't think. I just clapped my hands together over the flame. The crumbling, ashen wings fell and burst briefly into flame. The body twitched in the hot wax and a wind rushed in through the window and blew the candles out. The air grew thick. Something changed.

I can't remember the name or the face of my first love. I can't remember the color of my mother's eyes but I remember every detail of that night. The room spun like I was drunk. Katie threw her head back and laughed her musical laugh. Jared squeezed our hands and continued the chant. We felt power in the air. We'd struck a chord.

We got loud again that night, in our chanting and our later ecstasy, maybe louder than we'd ever been before. I'm sure we would have gotten complaints if not for the neighbors. Katherine walked naked to the window when she saw lights.

"They're taking that shithead away in cuffs and questioning his wife. She won't let go of her dog. I think I see blood. On the dog, not the wife. I don't think it's moving."

Her nipples became more pointed when she leaned forward to look at the scene, and the police lights turned her skin red and blue and red again.

"And they thought there was something wrong with us."

She ran a hand through her hair, turned away from the window, and came back to bed.

The next time we did a ritual it felt flat. It was good, but not as good as that night. They were beautiful, but not as beautiful as they seemed to me before. It just wasn't what I wanted anymore. It wasn't good enough. I'd had better. I wanted a feeling that wasn't there.

I thought I could see their disappointment, too, but I'm not sure. It might have just been me. I brought it up when we were done.

"Animal sacrifice is big in almost every religious tradition." Jared nodded at me. Katie pursed her lips. "It's an important step in our studies. It's a huge area of research and a taboo that prevents progress. If we want to get at the root of it all, we've got to come to terms with sacrifice."

Katie thought it was going too far. She was a vegetarian.

"Think of them as test animals," Jared said.

Katie wasn't having any of it. We stayed up all night pleading, but it was no good. She stood firm. She should be remembered for that. She refused to spill another creature's blood.

My teeth feel itchy, like they haven't been brushed in days. How long has it been? There's still something stuck back there. We used human teeth once, ground with a mortar and pestle until they were a thick, chalky wet powder. No appreciable results. They were all full of cavities. We got them from a dental student.

Jared's grandmother got worse. He kept to himself for a few days and didn't want to talk about it. Katie and I were worried about him. We stopped experimenting. Jared didn't even want sex. Katherine and I made love alone in that big bed when he went out for long walks.

He told us he was going to quit school and go home to take care of her, but one night when the phone rang he just knew. He didn't pick up.

It rang and rang, and he said, "She's gone."

He went home for the funeral that weekend and came back a mess.

All he did for weeks was cry, watch television, cook, and research. He threw himself into the rituals in a way he never had before, and we wanted to support him so we went along with it.

Late one night as the candles were sputtering out, Jared said, "If we could just find the right words, motions, and reagents, I know something incredible would happen. There can't be just this world.

I know there isn't. We're getting close now. We're going to find it."

Katherine and I were glad to see him excited about something.

Our instincts clarified. There were no measurable phenomena but our passions, so we gave ourselves to passion. When we all three felt the presence of power it was clear. We would lock eyes and smile. The world went quiet and we could see every detail and imperfection. Everything was in focus. We breathed with time and tasted thoughts. Colors were more clear, feelings, more intense. We moaned and thrashed and writhed and came.

When we weren't performing rituals, everything felt lessened. We spent all our excess time on preparation, documentation, or the basic requirements of our lives. Papers and old books formed tall, unruly piles in our apartment. None of us enrolled in classes for the spring. It was all about the work. I fell out of touch with everyone. When my parents called I didn't answer the phone.

We really thought we were going to change the world. We were going to open up a whole new field of study and destroy everyone's notion of what's real.

It was Jared urging us on, then, but it wasn't his fault. We were all there. I can't blame him any more than I blame myself. Still I can't help wondering if he somehow knew and didn't care. Maybe he even wanted it.

Jared reminded us of the meaning of sacrifice.

"It's got to be something we treasure," he said. "We've spent money and burned offerings, but we never gave of ourselves. We haven't bled for it."

"You mean literally or figuratively?" Katie asked.

"Was thinking literally. There's tons of traditions that do it, and I've got it all planned out if you're all right with it."

The plan was very specific but that was how we operated at the time. Sometimes we would collaborate and sometimes one of us would bring an idea before the group. Apart from the bloodletting, this was no more unusual than the rest. After a little online research we felt confident that we could cut to bleed but not deep enough to need bandages right away.

And then, two nights ago or a week ago or however long I have been waiting in the dark, remembering and forgetting and remembering again, we prepared for what would be our last ritual.

(Hypothesis: It was all one ritual that took seventeen months. The process was gradual. We gave up pieces of our lives and selves. We were the sacrifices.)

Katherine drew the symbols as she had so many times, but these were different. The angles were strange. They lacked symmetry. We lit fresh candles and watched the wicks blacken and curl. We burned a mixture of herbs that we had grown from seedlings. Smoke filled the room but we'd long since taken the batteries out of the alarm.

We spoke the words of dusty and forgotten tongues as if we were born to speak them: words of binding, words of power, words that open and words that close. There were lost and ancient names and more than a few. It all felt familiar. Our bodies moved naturally, as if guided by muscle memory. It felt like we had done all this before, like we were meant to do it.

It was a stone knife. It looked old. Part of me knew that Jared had made it. I'd seen him whetting it or I thought I had. I thought I remembered him chipping it out of a larger stone, but it looked too old for that to be true.

Jared went first, drawing the blade against his palm quickly and firmly. He closed his palm and beads of blood formed and dripped down the back of his hand. His blood had stained the edge of the blade red and I used that same edge to cut my hand. The pain was sharp but it felt like release. I passed the blade to Katherine. She gritted her teeth and cut.

Still chanting, we reached out and clasped our hands together, fingers entwined above the central fire. The drops sputtered in the eager flame. I saw another drop fall, slowly, from our entwined hands toward the fire and I blinked. When I opened my eyes again the room was perfectly still. We were all holding our breath.

I felt that moment stretch and pull, and then the streetlights outside shattered.

Jared started to laugh as the glass rained onto the pavement below. His head snapped backwards on his neck with a crack and the laugh turned from that gentle laugh I knew to something dark and vicious. I heard voices that weren't his pouring from his throat, right there with the laughter. A thousand voices joined in a language I had never known. They made noises no human voice could make: hollow, wet, and sharp.

Katherine screamed and Jared's head rolled to look her in the eye. Her scream cracked and split and hit a pitch that rang in my ears and dug into my head carrying pain without limit or restraint.

I closed my eyes. I said some words to the close and hungry darkness, and then I wept.

Even with my eyes closed I heard screaming. It sounded like millions screaming, like the whole world was in the room screaming into my ears. I saw my poor dead dog spread over three feet of concrete, his back legs still twitching. I saw my ex-girlfriend's face turn red, her tongue lolling from her mouth and eyes bulging, clawing at my hands that were locked around her throat. I saw the clear sky split apart and blanket the city in worms.

When I opened my eyes, sweet, beautiful Katherine was covered in blood. She still had the knife and she was shrieking as she stabbed Jared, over and over, though he was already a torn canvas of bloody wounds. She turned to me and I met her eyes. Only they weren't her eyes anymore.

There was nothing there. Not blackness. Blackness can be perceived. There's no way to show an absence with words or capture it on film. This was not-seeing, unknowing, the complete impossibility of understanding what might lurk behind those once-loved lashes. There was a sickening silence in those two pinpricks and beyond them only void.

I don't remember anything else from that night. I'm sure the police report is accurate; they must have arrived sometime after the screaming began and found the door open. They found his body, the candles, the ritual space, the blood. They told me I was easy to find. I'd left a trail of blood that they followed into the stairwell. I was holding the stone knife in slippery hands. I was chewing on something and choking and gibbering.

They told me later that his eyes were gone.

I asked them what happened to the notes but they wouldn't say. I told them they had to be destroyed but they wouldn't promise. I told them there was something stuck between my teeth but they wouldn't help.

Something traveled from Jared to Katherine when their eyes

met and then her eyes met mine. I've tried not to look anyone in the eye but it's too hard. I hope I'm dead before they put me in a courtroom. Too many bodies there. Too many eyes. Maybe I won't see a jury at all, just a padded cell and a locked door. But you have to believe me: I loved them. I never would have hurt them. She never would have done that. It wasn't her anymore.

It was waiting for us for so long. People like us. Curious minds to work out the patterns and dig up the truths beneath. Self-involved fools too blinded by ego to fear the implications of their study.

The only reason I'm still alive is because It wants me alive. I don't know why. Maybe It wants an audience. The court, the jury, the reporters, the cameras. They haven't left me any way to kill myself. Maybe I can put this pencil through my eye.

There is always something smaller and something larger. We didn't know there was a solar system before Galileo. We didn't know there was a quark before we divided the hadron. And yet we operate under the delusion that this universe is all there is. Of course there are other universes. Of course there are. Whether they are removed by space or time or stranger dimensional lines, the means for travel between them is performed in unspeakable ways.

Yes, that felt right. I'm getting close now. The truth rewards. Maybe It will let me sleep.

Perhaps I've done something terrible just by committing it all to paper. Thought, belief, words, power. Speaking as invocation and writing another spell. And what if this was the goal? Measured belief? Possibility? Potential spreading through the eyes but also the mind, eyes windows for words, the brain passages of thought and faith? It is here now, we have allowed it, seeking travel, intellect. Contagious.

Should I destroy these papers, stab out my eyes? Is the warning more valuable than the risk? I'm not sure I want you to believe me. I'm not sure which is worse, to let It roam this unsuspecting world or to pave the way for It to be recognized.

Whether herald or warning, I am sorry. I don't know what else to say. I don't know what else to do.

They never found her. She's still out there, or whatever's left of her. A shell, wandering the waiting streets, carrying the coming darkness.

Part and Counterpart

Jennifer Stern

Mornings, and other times when it's been awhile since the last drink, I think about the goats. About their white heads and the little skitters of gravel they loosen from the mountainside. About the stones kicked down at our excavation sites every year, the big ones that pierce the canvas tents through. Last summer, one of the postdocs took off his helmet near the quarry and a shard of rock got him just above the eye. The cut healed funny so that he looked like he carried a little tubular worm around on his forehead.

The goats plague the Burgess Shale, that collection of sap and carcass where, once a year, I bring the graduate students from my laboratory to collect fossils of trilobites and *Nectocaris* and *Opabinia*. The goats' eyes follow us from up high as we drill and unearth; they startle at our rock saws; they break our concentration.

Once, one of them stared me down behind the camp store as we walked past with boxes of crackers and beer and work we had printed from the little office area in the back.

He was grayish, a little frizzed at the ears. His beard was ridiculous. I couldn't make eye contact, but I threw him a cracker. He wasn't shy the way they're supposed to be. It had been a funny morning on account of a malfunction in the copy area of the camp store, and I wasn't surprised to see him hanging around.

The malfunction was partly my fault. Something stupid had gotten into me a few months prior while I was looking at an Excel spreadsheet of our data. I had arrowed down and past thousands of empty cells until I hit the ten-thousandth row and then the ten-thousandth column. It took probably fifteen minutes. In that faraway cell, which nobody would ever find, I wrote: *I am safe here.* That morning at the camp store, it was found. One of the students had gone to print the data, and the spreadsheet now thought it contained one hundred million cells. We stood at the printer and watched pages and pages fill with empty rectangles, until I finally removed the rest of the blank paper from the tray.

When I first told Beth about the goats, she offered me one of her Valium. She was my ex and the favored parent of our daughter. We were at a gathering after the funeral of someone Beth once knew. (According to Beth, I had known her, too, but this was exaggeration.) I had spent the last half hour watching groups form and disband and making my way through a sheet of nicotine gum.

Beth signaled the bartender and when he pretended not to see, she turned to me. "Just so you know," she said, "I wouldn't want to be cremated. If something were to happen."

I scratched my head and nodded. Beth and I hadn't been together for twelve years, and I really thought she should be giving this information to someone else, but I told her I'd keep it in mind. Just in case.

Then I said, "Nice flowers."

Beth went over to talk with the dead woman's family. She gestured with her good arm and as she leaned into a hug, her face was a picture not of grief but sympathy. They had lost touch years before.

I hadn't thought Beth would let her ankle brace show—since her stroke, she has gone to efforts to hide it under long pants or hippie skirts—but there it was, bunched underneath a pair of black tights as if daring someone to call attention to it. I still saw her twice a month, when I picked up our daughter Anna for the weekend. (When I dropped Anna back on Sunday nights, Beth would assure me that a twelve-year-old girl isn't supposed to like her father.) She had asked me to come that day because I met the dead woman at a party in college, but I'm chagrinned to say that I didn't remember, and that during the burial I was thinking about the coming meal and about how Angelo's was supposed to have the best ravioli in Chicago.

At the luncheon, I sat in Beth's blind spot—another residual from the stroke. We were at one of those big round tables that hold twelve, and her mother sat on the other side of her. I had watched as Beth sat down to see which side of her vision she would offer to me.

Waiters brought ravioli and bread and chicken parmesan and salad.

Beth was pretty, but she didn't know it. She had that thick hair that fell into waves at the ends, and her lips were a little too wide but in a pleasing way. Usually, she was convinced that her weak arm and stiff leg made her unattractive. But today, she didn't seem shy. There was something that livened her about all these people from college, all these people who had known her before the stroke.

I whispered to Beth that there was something obscene about all this food when the person of honor wasn't eating.

Her blind spot forced her to turn her head all the way toward me. She shrugged. "If we eat," she said, "Mia's family will eat."

Mia had come to a freak and tragic end. To my understanding, it had been from a virus caught from a mosquito at the surgical clinic where she worked three weeks a year outside of Tena, Ecuador. A rainforest mosquito; a transfer to a modern hospital that came too late. Septic shock.

I took a long drink of my gin.

"You're worrying," Beth said, with a little amused smile. She knew my habits.

"Me?" I asked. "What am I worrying about?"

"About whether there's something infectious in the air."

I snorted. "Eat your lunch."

Beth took a bite of ravioli. "I barely recognize Mia's sister."

"Things get busy," I said.

When I said this, she looked at me in a way that made me flush and stammer. From behind Beth's head, I saw her mother turning to look at me. Not frowning. Just watching me dead-on, like you would watch a monkey at the zoo when it starts to rain, curious how it will react. I fingered the nicotine gum in my pocket.

Rachel, my girlfriend, would have enjoyed this. She was always saying I was too busy. She didn't like that I was gone four weeks a year, or that when we watched TV, I would look over data from the lab on my computer. I'd look up, and she would ask when we were going to spend more time together, and I would remind her that we were sitting side by side and that our feet were touching.

She would have said, "No wonder your daughter doesn't talk to us."

We bumbled around Anna. Sometimes, you could see Rachel thinking up reasons to go to our bedroom and back, each time passing Anna's room, each time taking brief glances through the crack of her half-open door. Later, taking out her lipsticks and nail polishes and setting them out in front of Anna, like toy soldiers.

Then there was me—bringing Anna to the lab and showing her the cell culture. I would take down the model trilobite and explain that these animals lived five hundred million years ago, when fish swam in the seas but life on land was still confined to bugs, not long after that explosion of life that with time became turtles, and then birds, and then us. Anna would finger the model's shell and snort and say that she found something like that running around in the kitchen one night.

I would put the model away and wonder how to explain to her that I did not leave her mother because of the stroke; that it was the stroke that kept me with her mother those extra months after it was over; that I am not with Rachel because of her two strong arms and legs.

In bed later, Rachel would say, "Really, you can be so dense. What does a twelve-year-old girl want with a trilobite?"

Now, when I think about rainforest diseases, I think about how the Ebola in the news doesn't seem quite as scary when it occurs in a modern ICU with sterile facilities. (This also came to mind last week when that woman had a coughing fit at Bergstein's.) They say that the death rate is 60% and I have no reason not to believe them. I'm not in Public Health so I wouldn't know how to calculate a rate that is one number in Monrovia and, in Atlanta, another number entirely.

At the gathering, with a couple of drinks in her, Beth seemed to forget about her weakness. Her eyes glittered. She leaned in and whispered, "Meet me at the bar."

I followed her.

She turned and said, "My mother is listening to us. She looks like she's just eating her ravioli, right? But she's not. She's listening to every word we say."

"Your mother?" I smiled. "Yours? Imagine that."

Beth ordered a gin and tonic from the bar. She sloshed when she set her glass down. She said, "I was going to go with Mia on one of her trips to Ecuador. We always talked about that. But you know—" She waved her good hand at the weak side of her body.

"Well," I said, my voice congenial. "It's a good thing you didn't."

"She went every year," Beth said. "Most went just fine."

To make Beth feel better, I said, "The size of the insects down there—"

"—All that green." She took a last drink and set down her glass. "Can you give me a ride home?"

Beth left me at the bar and found Mia's sister to say goodbye. I watched them talk for a long time. Whatever she said, the woman didn't quite seem to agree. When Beth came back, I asked, "What did you say?"

"I said, we get past a certain age, we don't usually keep getting better."

Outside, we stood and blinked. It was one of those August days of liquid sun. Heat rose in squiggles from the streets. Beth put her hand on my arm as if for balance, but the sidewalk was easy and flat. She asked me if I remembered that long-since unfortunate incident with the butterscotch Schnapps. Or how the sunlight used to hit the Quad that semester we got stuck with the eight a.m. classes.

In return, I tried to miss the three years we had been together, in college and those months following. It wasn't coming. Her pregnancy during our senior year had cooled things between us. At the time, I was applying for graduate school in Evolutionary Biology and not thinking of much beyond the applications and the laboratory and how time came in layers—the Cambrian and the Devonian and the Carboniferous. One time layered on top of the next, so that what is important is not the singular animal but the progression of things.

Keeping Anna hadn't been my choice. When Beth told me, I had this picture of us moving out to the suburbs, of myself sitting out in the garage and drinking beer for something to do on Sunday afternoons. It weighed on me. But later, after Anna came, I would have been okay with it. Because of the way that she tried to suck her thumb, or the way she'd look just past you. That little birthmark on her foot.

It didn't happen.

Instead, the stroke happened. Beth moved the baby in with her mother for the extra help. They drew inward, and I continued to live in my studio in Hyde Park. Then, when Anna was six months old and sitting and making those noises she made, it hit me that we should be living together, and I went out and bought Beth a ring.

Beth said no. We were in the car outside of her mother's house, drinking rum and pineapple juice (though I'm not sure we opened the pineapple juice). We hadn't yet broken up. She said we weren't in love with each other.

I remember almost asking, isn't that beside the point by now?

And I remember my stomach wasn't right that night. I went through a sleeve of Rolaids. The meeting point of regret and relief did something funny to it. Or maybe it was the rum.

The lungfish is a funny creature: a fish that comes with a pair of lungs. It sounds like a toy that would be advertised between cartoons on Saturday mornings. But lungfish are real—you can see them at the Shedd Aquarium in Chicago. Today, they are confined mostly to swamps, but in earlier times, they walked—probably only a few feet here and there, but enough to see farther than they might. Nowadays, their lungs have a different purpose: when the swamps dry, they can sit among the remnants and breathe the air and survive the wait for rain. I wonder which of these two uses is the better, but I haven't decided yet.

After the funeral, at my laboratory—I needed to pick up a notebook on the way to drop Beth home—I told Beth I had the dream about the mountain goats again. In this one, they stood on the rock face and kicked silt into the quarry. There were five of them, and the little stones they stirred rained down over the alder and spruce, over the tents. It was like a storm made entirely of stones.

Beth was looking at the lab benches, fingering the microscope and the centrifuge. She said, "Something looks different."

"It's a different lab," I said. "They moved me a couple of years ago."

She gave a little embarrassed smile. "It's been awhile."

I told her that there were bits of soft tissue in these fossils that we looked at and if we could get to their DNA, we could compare them to other animals to see where they fit on the tree of life.

"Tree of life," Beth said. "Sounds religious."

I reddened. "The phylogenetic tree."

"Oh." Beth smiled. "That."

I watched her look through the photo albums. She turned the page. I looked over her shoulder and told her, "We're wrapping up fossils, there." Sometimes, I explained, you hammer through a rock and when it splits in two, you find parts of the same fossil on each side. The pieces fit back together like a hand in a glove, but you can't let them touch, or they grind each other down. So you wrap each piece in its own paper before you fit them back together to pack them away. You call them part and counterpart. Together, but for that layer of paper. Almost touching, but not.

Beth said, "I know some couples like that."

And at Bergstein's—because Beth needed a cup of coffee to get rid of the last remnants of the gin—Beth said, about Mia: "You met her once. You don't know it. (We were at that party at Todd's—remember him?) I called Mia after the stroke. She was out in New Mexico, in medical school, so I thought she'd be interested in the details. She had flowers delivered. (Remember those lilies? I told you that they were from my mother.)

"We talked for maybe an hour, and the whole time, her tone was hushed and apologetic, and finally I said, 'What's with your voice? You go to school in a hospital, you must see this shit every day.' And after a pause, she said that the people she saw with strokes came to her as people with strokes, and that the discomfort wasn't in the illness itself, it was in the transformation.

"Then we lost touch. It was my fault as much as hers. She called a couple more times and I let it go to voicemail. I should have picked up, or called her back. I wasn't too busy to talk. Sometimes I was eating dinner. Sometimes I was watching TV. The thing is, I didn't want to hear Mia's voice—she was right about the discomfort, and I didn't want to hear its transformation."

In return I told Beth a story: I had been in the hospital the year before. Anna didn't know. (And she doesn't need to.) I went to the emergency room for a pain in the chest. As the nurses were swarming in and out of the room, as I was being hooked up to the EKG machine, I thought: I have been waiting for this. For years. And now, thinking I was having the heart attack I had feared, there was a certain calm in realizing that my disaster was no longer impending, because it was already here.

It turned out to be a panic attack. They watched my heart overnight. In the morning, they sent in a psychiatrist who offered Paxil, but I declined.

Rachel took a week off of work—I remember, her PI hadn't been happy to lose a research scientist in the middle of a big experiment. She made chicken soup out of a recipe book. The garlic was almost coming out my pores. (That terrific, silly, serious expression she would get on her face.) It surprised me. That was three months before we moved in together. But I'm digressing.

Since, I've thought about that calm.

As I told Beth, we were eating rugelach and I was tonguing my teeth, sure that I had a stuck poppy seed somewhere. Beth was running her fork over her plate, batting at the leftover raisins, and when I mentioned Rachel, she accidently hit one off the plate.

When we were almost to Beth's house—past the Edens, up Touhy—I saw the park with the tube slides where Anna used to like to play when she was young. I had that feeling like I had eaten too much. I asked Beth, "You think she'll ever warm up again?"

"I'll talk to her," Beth said. "She needs to learn to be polite."

"Polite," I echoed, a little deflated. I fingered the nicotine gum in my pocket. There was nothing impolite about the way Anna would put on those earphones so as to not disturb us with her music. And that morning that she called to ask if she could stay with Beth instead of keeping her weekend with me, she had said both *please* and *thank you*.

"Don't tell me it's her age," I said.

"It's her age."

"She still likes you," I explained.

"I would hope so," Beth said. "I'm her mother."

The fruit markets had their peaches out in bins. There were cantaloupe and tomatoes and honeydew and plums, and bags of Taralli in the windows: fennel, I imagined, and sugar.

Beth's eyes followed them as we passed. "She says you don't talk much. You lecture instead."

I drummed my fingers on the steering wheel.

Beth continued to look out the window. "They said Mia was brilliant," she said after a time. "I played along."

"Played along?" I put on my turn signal.

"Don't you think," Beth said, "That a truly brilliant doctor would know how not to get herself infected?"

I gave a little laugh. "That's harsh."

Beth was quiet after that. At the red light, I noticed something in her face—a funny look, somewhere between outrage and resignation. I could tell she thought I was taking sides against her. It surprised me. In retrospect, I think she wanted me to tell her that you do not have to climb and travel to be brilliant.

We had the windows down, and I could smell the sugar from the Russian bakery. It was mixed with the heat, a sticky smell that put a sourness in the mouth in compensation. Beth's hair was stringy from the wind. A single strand clung to the corner of her mouth. It looked uncomfortable, so I pushed it behind her ear.

When we pulled up in front of her house, the sun was starting to go down. It was setting earlier now, and the mornings were cooler. Beth watched the light glint off the dash. I turned off the ignition. It should have been awkward, sitting in the same spot where I had proposed twelve years before.

I said, "Remember that cheap rum we were drinking?"

She smiled. "You were wearing those ridiculous glasses."

"Ridiculous?" I said. "They actually weren't—"

"And your hair was longer," Beth said. "I always liked all that hair."

We sat. I leaned my seat back and Beth leaned her seat back, and we looked up at the car ceiling in lieu of the sky. Red undertones came through the windows. They softened Beth's face. I put my head next to hers, close.

Then, she did the oddest thing. She sat her chair up and twisted away to face out her window. The back of her shoulders stiffened. Her voice, now with sharp inflections: "Don't you have a girlfriend?"

"Of course," I said.

"You wouldn't think it."

I startled and sat up. "Whoa—" I said. "—I wasn't going to—"

But I could tell that she wanted to believe that we were going to. That she appealed. She had her head turned away, but through her wing mirror I could see a reflection of her face, its satisfaction.

I thought for a minute and then said, for her sake: "You're the one who said no."

She opened the car door and maneuvered out, and I watched her move toward the house. Then I turned on the ignition and chewed more nicotine gum and pulled away from the curb fast as she disappeared inside.

Up around the Walcott Quarry, the air is thin and everything is on a diagonal. You stand at a diagonal. It gets to you at first. Later, you think it's otherworldly, and then with time, 'other' becomes everywhere else. But 'other' is a thing that depends on more than just distance—Hyde Park is no longer forest; its dragonflies are no longer the size of crows; its trees are not yet coal. It's funny how time comes in layers.

I mentioned this to Rachel once. We were out near the Quadrangles, huddling against winter air. She was holding a coffee that steamed in our faces. Her nose was red. In response, she said, "Cakes come in layers." I'm still not sure what her point was with this, but it did remind me that her birthday was coming up and that I hadn't yet gotten her a present.

Then Rachel said something and laughed, and I laughed, too. I had missed what she said, but we were laughing together, and it was nice. I held her hand, although I couldn't feel it well through the mitten. She gave me a drink of her coffee.

I had this fleeting picture of the two of us hanging out in the Paleocene. There would be no humans or dogs or antelope, just birds and mammals the size of mice. We'd build a house out of sticks and then all we'd have to do is look up through the ceiling at dappled sun. I didn't tell her, of course. She wouldn't go for that, and there are some things you just don't say.

Here is another thing you don't say: I spied on Beth and Anna once. They were at the Ghirardelli's down by the Water Tower, that summer that the Cows on Parade exhibit lined Michigan Avenue. Anna was five. She had just gotten the ordering thing down. Every time Beth would try to talk to the cashier, Anna would interrupt and ask her what flavor she wanted, and then she'd turn to the girl behind the counter and say, *She'll have hot fudge*. I watched Beth's hand graze Anna's head and the way Anna would jostle her with her hip. I was going to wave but something stopped me, some need to know if they would see me even if I didn't move. Later, after they had come and gone, I ordered a cup of vanilla to earn my table.

I didn't think about it later. It didn't creep in, what with all the work at the lab. All those specimens, each taking the greatest concentration—the fossil is the weakest part of rock, after all, the most likely to fracture with a hammer and chisel. I thought about worlds other creatures came from: the Jurassic; the Carboniferous. I needed these worlds to be bigger than me, to tamp down my little agonies, to keep them small.

Something Beth said after the funeral niggled at me, though. I brought it up to Anna years afterward, when she was seventeen.

Rachel and I were married by then, and she was waiting for us at home. Anna and I were on a long walk through the city, from Foster down to Hyde Park. Our feet ached and our fingertips were freezing. At one point, Rachel called my cell to say she would spring for a cab and I told her I'd pick her up some of that vinegar she likes on the walk home.

What I asked Anna was this: "I talk to you, don't I?"

Anna got a little smile on her face as if sharing a joke with herself, but she nodded. I remember we were down past Roosevelt, past the Congress Hotel. We watched busses splash through the buildup of gray water at the curbs. On the next block, in some tacit agreement, Anna said, "Tell me a story."

I told her that I couldn't get the goat problem figured out. How it had weighed on me since the climb to my first dig site. The trail was steep, and at first the goats were just little skitters of movement among the spruce. Later, they came closer, or maybe we came closer to them. Our PI called to us to put on our helmets, but not believing I'd need a helmet to walk a trail, I had packed it in one of the trunks that would arrive by helicopter the next day.

"Did you get kicked?" Anna asked, and when I said I didn't, she wrinkled her forehead like she wasn't sure what the problem was.

Then we walked on and shared the sounds of the taxis and the L and the tinkling of the Salvation Army canisters.

I didn't say that on that first climb, I had left a six-month-old baby and a girlfriend with a stroke back in Chicago. Or that I had thought to take those weeks and simplify, but when I saw the goats—the multitude of them—it seemed there was only so much chaos I could leave behind.

Instead, as we walked, I pictured the rocks, their shards and remnants. The circle of the tents.

And the nights. I didn't sleep well, then. I'd wake after a few hours and sit outside and chain-smoke Camel Lights. The trees black against purple; the cold almost singeing the lungs. At the time, I had assumed it would be my only excavation—I would propose to Beth when I got home—and I had figured that after she said yes, I would leave graduate school for something more practical.

And the plans—that I would teach Anna to pick out Orion and Sagittarius. That I would take her to eat ice cream on Friday afternoons. That I would sit out in the backyard and watch her dig a hole with her toy shovel, because some other kid had told her that with enough effort, you can dig all the way through to China. I'd decide not to tell her that it wasn't going to happen. Or that the next summer, I would fill her work back in with a bag of soil from Menards. Instead, I'd sit beside her and empty out her bucket, and we'd peer down and try to see things as they could be.

CPSIA information can be obtained
at www.ICGtesting.com
Printed in the USA
FSOW03n0442280915
11486FS

9 780985 340735